KT-389-753

TOM RIDER'S RECKONING

In prosperous El Cobarde, the respected sheriff Tom Rider is happily anticipating his retirement. But, barely hours after Tom hands over the reins of command, notorious local lawbreaker Jeb Deeds escapes from his prison train and storms the streets with dynamite, pursuing a vendetta against the eminent town founders. For a long-buried secret is about to emerge, and Deeds intends to bring a bloody reckoning to this town built on foundations of murder and treachery . . .

ROB HILL

TOM RIDER'S RECKONING

Complete and Unabridged

LINFORD
Leicester

First published in Great Britain in 2013 by
Robert Hale Limited
London

First Linford Edition
published 2015
by arrangement with
Robert Hale Limited
London

A catalogue record for this book is available
from the British Library.

ISBN 978–1–4448–2320–2

Published by
F. A. Thorpe (Publishing)
Anstey, Leicestershire

Set by Words & Graphics Ltd.
Anstey, Leicestershire
Printed and bound in Great Britain by
T. J. International Ltd., Padstow, Cornwall

This book is printed on acid-free paper

For Val and Joss

Prologue

As the Butterfield approached, the men pulled kerchiefs up over their faces and swung their horses out into the road. There were three of them. They were dressed in work clothes: cotton shirts which had seen better days, dust-covered hats, and two of them wore leather chaps. They rode cheap cow ponies they had bought from some itinerant trader.

The men were nervous. They didn't speak. Instead, they exchanged sidelong glances as each one kept a check on the reaction of the others. All of them were in their thirties, part of the generation that had done their growing up during the war and were accustomed to fighting for what they wanted. They drew their Colts and checked the chambers.

Here, the land was flat and dry. The

ash-white desert sand was dotted with patches of switchgrass and displays of beaver-tail cactus. Occasional stands of scrub oak broke the horizon. The river was a mile away; it was not visible from this distance but its path was indicated by the tops of the line of screw beans and river walnuts which ran beside its banks. Along the horizon to the north the Trans Pecos were purple behind the heat haze, which had already collected even though it was not yet midday.

The road was on the Butterfield route from Kansas to the small towns in the south of Texas. The stage slowed on this section, ready to halt at the designated stop-off at El Cobarde, where passengers broke the journey and fresh horses were supposed to be available. The men had been following the progress of the stage by the cloud of silver dust thrown up behind it.

'What if he shoots at us?'

The man who spoke looked poorer than the other two. His shirt was torn and his hat was dirty and misshapen.

His chaps were the old-fashioned Mexican kind and did not fit him properly.

The stage started to slow. The driver and the guard peered forward at the men lined up across the road.

'Last guy didn't,' one of the others snapped. 'They don't get paid enough.'

This man appeared to be in charge. He was the heaviest built of the three; waiting in the morning heat had made him irritable.

'They've read about those west Texas gangs in the newspapers, the fellas who shoot you for looking at 'em wrong,' the third man added. 'They're scared we're gonna do that.'

When the Butterfield was 200 hundred yards away one of the men walked his horse forward a couple of paces and raised his arm to halt the coach. The driver leaned forward in his seat, lashed the reins and drove straight at him. The guard reached behind him and lifted a rifle to his shoulder.

The three riders pulled their horses

off the road as the first shot from the guard's Winchester whined over their heads. One of them fired back. They separated, circled wide and came up behind the coach.

The driver drove the team hard. The horses stampeded forward, the traces rattled and the wooden wheels spun. The cloud of dust swelled as the coach speeded up.

The guard spreadeagled himself on the roof and fired blind into the dust cloud. The riders shot back; their bullets slammed into the back of the Butterfield.

Then the leading rider spurred his horse, swung wide to overtake and drew level with the driver. At first the man didn't see him. He was an old guy, experienced at his work. He leaned half-out of his seat with the reins at ease in his hands, intent on coaxing wings out of the team.

The horses powered forward. At a wild gallop, staring-eyed, their manes thrashed; foam flecked their mouths.

Every rivet in the Butterfield rattled; the hard ground shuddered the rigid axle until the whole coach seemed as if it was going to burst apart.

The rider raised his Colt. The driver suddenly noticed him; panic crossed his face. The guard turned and tried to get him in his sights but the angle was awkward; he shot wide.

The rider steadied his aim, fired and caught the driver in the shoulder. The man threw himself to one side, screamed something to the guard and hauled on the reins. The horses bucked and twisted; the Butterfield lurched crazily. For a moment it looked as though it was going to crash over onto its side.

The riders following the coach hailstormed gunfire over the head of the guard. The rider up ahead drew alongside the lead pair, seized their reins and hauled on them to hinder the team. He called out to calm the terrified animals; their speed eventually slackened and slowed to a halt.

As soon as the Butterfield was still the guard jumped up, threw down his Winchester as if it burned him and raised his hands above his head.

'Strongbox is inside,' he yelled. 'Take it. We won't say nothing.'

One of the men who had followed the coach kept him covered while the others jumped down and yanked open the door.

The driver pulled himself upright. He gripped his arm; blood welled through his fingers. Pain twisted his face.

'Arm's busted,' he gasped. 'Ain't you gonna do something?'

The rider who had slowed the team waved for the guard to help him.

There was a shout from inside the coach.

'Box is mighty heavy.'

The other rider had dismounted now. Between them, they lifted the strongbox down onto the ground.

'Your lucky day, boys,' the guard said. 'You're looking at a shipment from the Town and City in Kansas.'

6

'Key?' one of them snapped.

'They don't give us the key,' the guard said. 'Bank keeps it.'

The rider at the head of the team let go of the bridles, climbed down from his saddle and shot the lock off the box. He threw open the lid and stepped back. The chest was full of cigar-sized rolls of coins wrapped in blue paper printed with the words 'Property of the Town and City Bank'. He broke one open. The mask disguised the smile which broke over his face. Gold coins fell into the palm of his hand, each one stamped with the twin-headed eagle and the provenance: 'Carson City'.

One of them gave a long whistle.

'We won't say nothing,' the guard added hastily.

The lead rider rounded on him.

'Yes you will. You tell everybody you was held up by the Fletcher boys from West Texas.'

'You're the Fletcher Gang?' The man's voice trembled. 'I thought there was more of you than this.'

The rider raised his .45.

'Make sure you tell everybody,' he said. 'Butterfields, the bank, everybody.'

'I will.' The guard nodded furiously. 'You got my word.'

The rider picked up the guard's rifle.

'Now go,' he said.

The guard shoved the driver to one side and grabbed the reins. As the wagon lurched forward he didn't look back.

The men heaved the box up onto the saddle of one of the horses.

'We'll do what we agreed,' the first rider said. 'Head out to the river where the ground is soft, bury it and leave it buried for a long while. There's enough here to set all three of us up for life.'

'Reckon they believed we were the Fletchers?'

The leader handed a single gold piece to each of the others and slipped one into his pocket.

'Souvenir.'

The other two gripped the coins in their teeth for a moment, examined them and smiled.

'They'll be telling everyone how all ten of the Fletcher Gang attacked 'em, how there was a blazing gunfight and how they were chased for miles. Main thing is that when Town and City set a reward, the bounty hunters start looking in West Texas and not around here.'

As the Butterfield disappeared into the distance, the men pulled the kerchiefs off their faces. Their grins were a mile wide.

1

Ten Years Later

As it was long past sundown, oil lamps in fancy glass shades bathed the Texas Rose saloon in lucent golden light. The pride of the place was a vast crystal chandelier, which sparkled at the centre of the high ceiling. Ox-blood velvet seats lined the walls; the long bar was cut from a single piece of oak; the brass foot-rail and spittoons were buffed to a shine; rows of glasses shone on mirrored shelves. Groups of poker players hunched over polished tables; in the far corner someone sat at a baby grand piano and tinkled out a sweet old tune.

Sheriff Tom Rider stood in his usual place. Tall, square-shouldered, with grey hair and a lined, weathered face, he wore a dusty Stetson, work shirt and

10

a pair of Peacemakers in his holsters. He rested one arm on the bar and surveyed the room with the self-assurance of a popular man, someone who knows that at the end of each day he will be respected for a job well done. A glass of water with a chunk of lemon in it waited at his elbow.

Three men were with him: Mayor Brogan, Doc Andrews and Bill Gifford, a ranch owner from out of town. They were well dressed in new hats and pressed linen shirts and smiled with the satisfaction that wealth brings. In their hands they nursed tumblers of rye; their gunbelts hung on pegs just inside the door.

'Gonna be mighty strange without you, Tom,' Brogan said.

He stood his glass on the bar and hooked a thumb in his vest pocket. An impressive gold watch chain looped across his round belly.

'El Cobarde may be small but it owes you big time. This was a rough cow town when you arrived. Took a

11

courageous man to straighten it out.'

Tom's work as a company engineer, charged with taking preliminary surveys for the railroad, had brought him here. But when he fell for Elizabeth Light, the daughter of an itinerant horse dealer, and heard of her ambition to stay in one place and open a school, he decided to put down roots.

Tom looked into the faces of his friends. Ten years ago, shortly before the railhead was built, they had appointed him sheriff. He was never afraid to take on local crooks, pursue rustlers and pacify bar fights. El Cobarde was orderly today because of him.

It had been an exciting time. That year Brogan and Gifford were starting to build the town on the old Butterfield route which connected Kansas with the small towns in the south of the state. They chose the site of an old Mexican village, where there was already a supply of fresh water. It was ideal longhorn country; they knew that a direct railroad link to the stockyards would make it rich.

Tom's appointment was an easy choice. Everyone respected his authority; his sense of fairness was well known; he was physically brave and accurate with a gun. More than that, he was unaffected by rumour and gossip; he treated people as he found them. He had no history in the place.

'Gonna have a drink tomorrow?' Brogan said.

The others laughed. On his appointment Thomas had forsworn hard liquor and had kept his word. Although the men often teased him about this, their respect for the sheriff was palpable.

'What will you do with yourself, Tom?' Gifford said. 'Hope you ain't thinking of going into the cattle business.'

Tom smiled.

'Reason I'm quitting is because of my knees. I can't go on climbing on an' off horses and running after young tearaways like I used to. Carpentry work needs doing on the house. Guess I'll start with that. Some of those jobs have been waiting fifteen years.'

Brogan and the others looked aside. Mention of the house made them uncomfortable. Tom had started building the place for himself and his new wife on the riverside plot that Gifford provided for him when he took the sheriff's job. Tom never finished it. He quit the construction work when Elizabeth died and never lived there. Even now, anyone who rode past could see the half-built porch and places where shingles had never been attached to the roof.

'Planning to move out there?'

Bill Gifford spoke. Concern for his friend was in his face. Bill also was a widower and understood loneliness. He was content on his ranch with his son and his grand-children, but he worried about Tom returning to the half-built house out there on his own. But there was no point in trying to dissuade him; Gifford knew what

Tom's answer would be.

'Can't live in the saloon for ever,' Tom said.

'What time's the train?' Brogan broke in to change the subject.

The men all looked up at the clock above the bar.

'Midnight,' Tom said.

'Must feel good, putting that lowlife behind bars,' Brogan went on.

'Jeb Deeds has been in and out of jail since he was thirteen,' Gifford said. 'Last time they let him out he hid out in a cave. Three months later him and his brothers were rustling my steers again. Pity you only caught Jeb and the other two got away. If there was any justice they'd all be at the end of a rope.'

'Can't hang a man for cattle-rustling no more,' Tom said.

'He shot at you when you went after him, didn't he?' Gifford said. 'Would have killed you if he could.'

'Their ma died when they were knee high,' Doc Andrews reflected. 'Then with what happened to his pa, the boys never had a chance.'

'Bull,' Brogan said sourly. 'Their sister looked after them, even taught them to read and write. That gave 'em the edge over a lot of fellas round here. On top of that, Bill let them stay on his land for no rent after their pa passed.'

'Mayor's right. It's a good way for you to go out, Tom,' Gifford said. 'We're all mighty grateful.'

The others murmured agreement.

'Soon as you and the deputy have got Deeds on the prison train, get some shut-eye,' Brogan said. 'We got a surprise for you tomorrow.'

Tom coloured. 'Surprise?'

'A party in your honour,' Brogan said. 'Whole town's invited.'

'I was intending to head on home.' Tom stared at his feet. 'Ain't much of a one for socializing.'

'Nonsense,' Brogan said. 'We've got to swear in the next sheriff and you've got to give the town a chance to show you how grateful they are.'

16

'That's kind of you,' Tom said. 'I can see that.'

'You're gonna have your picture took and Lawrence from the *Herald* will ask you a few questions.'

Tom smiled. 'An interview?'

'Nothing like that,' Brogan said. 'Just a few questions about how the town's changed, some of the arrests you've made. You know the kind of thing people are interested in.'

'Done my job, that's all,' Tom said.

The men laughed. They knew Tom well and expected a show of modesty.

'I got to ask something one more time,' Tom said.

Mayor Brogan sighed. He knew what was coming.

'You're quite sure you got the right man for the next sheriff?'

'We've been over this,' Brogan said. 'Brett is your deputy. He's the obvious choice.'

'We know you've got reservations, Tom,' Gifford said. 'That's only natural.'

'The town has grown,' Tom said. 'Brett is young.'

Mayor Brogan laughed. 'If that's all it is — '

'The boy's a hothead. He jumps before he thinks. He ain't thorough.' Tom looked the mayor in the eye. 'Brett is your son, Brogan. Don't reckon you'd appoint him if he wasn't.'

'It's potential that counts,' Gifford broke in hastily. 'When you make an appointment like this you try to see how good someone will be in the future. Who he's related to don't matter a hang.'

Doc Andrews agreed. 'Brett knows the place like the back of his hand and he's had you to show him how things are done. He's got a girl, so he ain't about to disappear over the horizon. Got a vested interest in the place.'

'Besides,' Gifford added. 'We all trust the mayor and he knows his boy better than anyone.'

'What about Ellie?' Tom said.

'Brett's girl? She's a real beauty,

crack shot with a rifle and a good horsewoman. She ain't dumb neither,' Brogan said. 'And I know what you're thinking.'

Tom said nothing.

'So what if she's Jeb Deeds's sister?' Brogan continued. 'You gonna hold a girl to account for what her brother and pa have done?'

'How's Brett gonna feel as he escorts the guy who's lined up to be his brother-in-law to the jail train tonight?' Tom said.

Brogan fired back his whiskey and slammed his glass on the bar.

'Brett's young. He's got to prove himself like we all had to. Are you saying he's no good?' Brogan said. 'Anyway, I'm mayor. He'll have me behind him.'

'Ellie won't blame Brett because her brother's in jail, Tom,' Gifford said. 'It wasn't Brett who put him there, it was you.'

An uneasy silence hung between the four of them.

'Where is Ellie, anyway?' Gifford said innocently. 'Ain't seen her all week. She and Brett were due to come out to the ranch on Sunday to see Johnny and the kids.'

Brogan stared into his whiskey.

'She ain't feeling well.'

Gifford waited for him to explain.

'She's upset.'

Brogan turned the glass in his hand.

'Her dog bit Brett. He had to shoot it.'

'Ranger?' Gifford said. 'He's a fine dog. Never knowed him bite anyone.'

'She hadn't trained him right,' Brogan said. 'Couldn't have.'

'I got to get back to the sheriff's office,' Tom said. 'Brett should have the prisoner ready. Train's due in half an hour.'

Outside, the street was lit by torches in iron stands outside the doors to the buildings. Even this close to midnight the air was warm. A few people were still about. Men tipped their hats to Tom and women waved. This party was going to be a bigger affair than he realized.

Tom had built the sheriff's office himself. When he moved into the saloon he no longer had a use for the timber that was lying round at home.

The office was a single room containing a desk, chairs and a rack for the Winchesters. Paperwork was strewn untidily across the desk. There was no one there. Through a doorway in the rear wall was a stone-built cell with a single window. Moonlight cut through the bars and cast long shadows across the body of Jeb Deeds, who lay on a wooden bench with his hat over his face.

As Tom started to tidy the papers on the desk, the door to the street burst open. Brett stood there, out of breath. His hat was tipped rakishly back on his head and an embarrassed grin lit his handsome face. A deputy's star was pinned to his shirt.

'I was just comin' to do that,' he said. 'Thought you'd be in the saloon with all the old guys.'

'Train's due,' Tom said. 'You should have got this ready.'

Brett's face coloured. He held his smile in place.

'Guess this is the last time you'll be telling me what to do.'

'Guess it is,' Tom said.

Bret reached up and unhooked the pair of iron shackles which hung on the wall beside the Winchesters. The cuffs weighed five pounds each and the chain that linked them was another five. Brett took a hoop of iron keys from a nail on the wall and unlocked the cell.

The man lying on the bench did not stir. Brett jabbed him with the toe of his boot.

'Hey.'

Jeb pushed the hat off his face.

'Easy, Brett. No need for that.'

He sat up and made a show of brushing down the sleeves of his shirt.

'No need for those things neither,' he said, gesturing to the shackles. 'I ain't going nowhere.'

'Prison regulations,' Tom interrupted. 'Stop wasting time.'

Jeb got slowly to his feet and stretched out his arms. Brett clamped the shackles on each of Jeb's wrists and fumbled for the key.

Watching the two young men face each other, Tom knew he was right. Even though Brett had the authority of the law on his side and Tom ready to back him up, he was nervous. He let Jeb take his time standing up; he was too slow finding the key. Tom figured Brett had been late because he had been putting off the moment when he had to enter Jeb's cell and do this. Brett slid the keys round the hoop.

'Lost the key?' Jeb said.

The keys slipped through Brett's fingers.

'See, if you weren't my sister's fancy man I wouldn't oblige by standing here with these irons on my wrists, waiting for you to lock them in place.'

Just as Brett found the right key Jeb

dropped his arms and the shackles clattered to the floor. A smile tightened his mouth.

'Irons are so heavy,' Jeb said. 'Sometimes they slip right off.'

Brett took a pace backwards.

'Pick 'em up.'

'Sure,' Jeb said.

Tom strode into the cell and shoved Jeb back down on the bench. He gathered up the shackles and held them on Jeb's wrists while Brett turned the key. Jeb went on with his ironic commentary.

'Takes two lawmen to shackle one prisoner. Even told you I wasn't minded to run off.'

Tom ignored him but Brett's hand shook.

Just as they finished, there was a tremor underfoot and a line of mortar dust fell from the cell ceiling. From somewhere far away they heard an approaching train. In the office, Tom gathered the paperwork off the desk, shuffled it into an envelope and led them out into the street where their horses waited.

The railhead was less than a mile outside town. Orange light from brush-wood torches dipped in tar lit the way for the passengers. The night air smelled of oil and wood-smoke. The engine pounded in the darkness as the driver built up a head of steam. Tom and Brett frogmarched Jeb through the crowd. Jeb searched their faces for someone who would acknowledge him; everyone knew him and they all turned away.

The railhead was frantic with activity. At the rear of the train shouts and whistles of the stockmen mingled with the fright-ened cries of the longhorns; the animals' hoofs clattered over wooden boards as cowboys from the ranches loaded the cattle trucks. In the middle section, rail-men handed down parcels and packing cases from a covered truck. Behind the engine were the passenger cars. Men and women pulled themselves up the narrow ladders and shoved luggage in through the open windows. Two screams from the guard's whistle cut through the din. Everyone hurried what they were doing.

Jeb turned to Tom.

'Done a good job, Sheriff. You can retire a happy man.'

'Shut up,' Tom said.

Jeb caught Brett's eye.

'Now you've got my sister's beau to carry on your good work. Must make you proud.'

'I caught you rustling cattle fair and square,' Tom said. 'Even found the irons you'd been using to change the brands. You were convicted by a jury and sentenced by a judge. You ain't got no one to blame but yourself.'

A cloud of steam exploded from under the engine. The driver leaned out of the cab and shouted something to the guard.

The men had finished unloading the truck now and gestured for Jeb to be brought up. Tom and Brett marched him up the ramp and held him while one of the railmen looped a chain through Jeb's shackles and padlocked it to the iron bar which ran the length of the truck. It was dark inside and empty apart from a wooden chair in the corner nearest the door. Flickers of torchlight danced across the wooden walls and shouts echoed. The guard's whistle screamed again and steam from the engine punched the air.

Brett was first down the ramp as soon as Jeb was chained. The railman followed. A man in a prison guard's uniform elbowed his way through the crowd and heaved himself up into the wagon. He was heavily built, unsmiling and moved awkwardly; he carried a shotgun under his arm.

He shoved Jeb to one side, pulled on the chains to check they were secure and gestured him to move to the far end of the truck.

'Sit on the floor,' he barked. 'Stand up before we get there and you'll start your time with a belly full of lead.'

The guard turned to Thomas.

'Papers?'

Thomas handed him the envelope. The guard grunted and stuck it inside his jacket. Jeb's chains rattled as he sat on the floor. Outside, the engine whistle shrieked.

'Counting on not seeing me again, Sheriff?' Jeb jeered.

'I'm counting on you doing your time, that's all,' Tom said.

Jeb laughed.

As Tom climbed out of the truck, he heard Jeb gasp with pain as the guard jabbed him in the gut with the stock of his shotgun.

2

Next morning Tom watched from the window of the sheriff's office as the town prepared itself to say goodbye to him. Men climbed up ladders to loop red, white and blue bunting across the front of the saloon and hang a canvas sign emblazoned with the words **Thomas Rider, Sheriff 1870-1880** across the square between the grocery and the livery stable.

People came and went from the saloon all morning. Women were weighed down with gingham-covered baskets; men laboured under chairs and trestles. Mayor Brogan appeared on the saloon porch at one point to encourage everyone to hurry along.

In the sheriff's office, Tom took down the Certificate of Investiture from the wall behind his desk. Elizabeth had framed it for him under glass soon after he was appointed. Written in swirling calligraphy, it was an impressive document. It carried the official blood-red seal of the State of Texas, Mayor Brogan's signature and the countersignature of the Governor. Thomas hadn't paid any attention to it in years. Apart from his coffee pot, it would be the only thing he took home with him from the office.

A row of leather-bound record books were shelved to one side of the sheriff's desk. Year on year, Tom had detailed the disputes he settled, the arrests he made and the judgments of the visiting court. The latest volume lay open at a blank page on his desk. A steel-nibbed pen, china inkwell and well-used blotter stood beside it. His last entry would be to record the dispatch of Jeb Deeds up the line.

Tom recognized that, like many of the guys he had brought to justice, the cards had been stacked against Jeb from birth. A few years after the war ended his widowed father had drifted to El

Cobarde with his nine-year-old daughter, Ellie, five-year-old twins, Luke and William, and four-year-old son, Jeb. Between them, they owned a covered wagon, two mules and the clothes they stood up in.

Hank Deeds teamed up with Bill Gifford, who lived with his wife and son on a land claim a few miles south. For some time Hank became his right-hand man. He helped him do whatever was necessary to put together a herd and found a ranch. Through Gifford he got to know Brogan and worked on some of the first buildings in El Cobarde when the place was just a stop-off on the Butterfield route south.

Weighed down with the strain of struggling to provide for his children and the frustration of never having enough money to roll up a stake of his own, Deeds had a reputation as a drunk by the time Tom arrived in town. The family lived in a tumbledown shebang on a corner of the Gifford spread, with Ellie doing all the chores.

That was the year Hank Deeds died and left Ellie to bring up her brothers. With Bill Gifford's wife taking her under her wing, she managed it. The little girl was intelligent, resourceful and tough.

Ellie did everything for Jeb and the twins. When Mary Gifford taught her how to cook, she cooked their meals; when Mary taught her how to sew, Ellie made their clothes; when she learned how to read, Ellie taught them their letters.

Despite their sister's best efforts, the boys ran wild. As children they were light-fingered in the store; as young teenagers they picked fights; later they tried their hands at cattle-rustling.

The townsfolk were contemptuous and a little afraid of these unruly, untrustworthy boys. They knew about Mary Gifford's best efforts and that Bill let them have the house rent free. They recalled that Hank Deeds had ended up as a hopeless drunk, as if the children were somehow to blame for that; they held Ellie responsible for failing to make her brothers appreciate the Giffords' kindnesses and for letting them stray from the straight and narrow.

With an acreage the size of the Gifford place, it was easy to cut a few head from the herd, drive them over to a neighbouring ranch and sell them. Everyone knew the Deeds brothers had been up to this for years. At their last attempt Tom caught Jeb red-handed. The twins gave him the slip and headed off to hole up somewhere in caves in the foothills of the Trans Pecos.

* * *

The door to the sheriff's office opened. The sound of urgent hammering from out in the street filled the room. Lawrence Carter stood there, a thin, nervous man in a bootlace tie, silver shirtbands and ink-spattered sleeves. He held a notebook.

'Expecting me, Sheriff?'

Across the street men on the ladders were nailing a line of fat rosettes over the saloon door. Another banner lay in the street, waiting to be hung.

Tom indicated the chair facing his desk. Lawrence fumbled with the pages of the notebook.

'Come to ask me some questions?' Tom tried to put Lawrence at his ease.

'Mayor Brogan asked me to write a profile for the *Herald* to go alongside a piece on the new sheriff.'

Lawrence seemed to be fighting pages of the book.

'Let's make it quick,' Tom said briefly. 'People know what I've done.'

'Ain't that, Sheriff,' Lawrence said.

He pulled a dirty piece of folded paper from between the pages of the notebook. 'Someone pushed this under the door of the *Herald* office.'

His hand shook as he passed it across the desk.

The paper read:

Lawrence Carter. Print this in the

Herald *or we will scatter your brains against a wall. Time has come for a reckoning. El Cobarde is founded on lies and corruption. Justice will be done.*

'They said — ' Lawrence began.

'I can see what they said,' Tom snapped.

He pushed his chair back, stood up and stared out of the window. The men were climbing their ladders to lift the second banner into place.

'Guess you better print it.' Tom turned to face Lawrence. 'That way your brains will stay where they belong.'

'It's the Deeds boys, ain't it?' Lawrence said.

'Ain't Jeb,' Tom said. 'That's for sure.'

Tom turned back to the window. The banner was unfurled over the street now: **Welcome Sheriff Brogan**.

'Can I ask you ... ?' Lawrence began.

'You don't need to ask me anything,'

Tom said. 'You've been writing copy for the *Herald* as long as I've been sheriff. If you want to pen-portrait me, go right ahead.'

Tom glanced down at the paper in his hand and frowned.

'I'll keep this for the time being. You've got no idea who slipped it under the door?'

Lawrence shook his head. 'It was there when I unlocked the office this morning.' He got to his feet. 'Sheriff, you don't reckon . . . ?'

'Don't you worry, Lawrence. Just print the message.'

Across the street Brett was standing on the saloon porch supervising the men putting up the banner. From the look of things he wanted his name higher.

Tom followed Lawrence out of the office and crossed the street to the saloon. Beaming, Brett held his arms wide.

'Whoa! You ain't allowed in here till noon. They're prettying up the place and want it to be a surprise.'

'Need to talk,' Tom said.

'No business today.' Brett grinned. 'Ain't allowed. Town's throwing a party for us. I'm in, you're out.'

'You ain't been sworn yet,' Tom said. 'Until you are, I'm sheriff. I got something to show you in the office, so come on.'

Brett's grin fell from his face.

'I'm sick of you orderin' me around. After today I don't take orders from no one.'

Brett strode down the porch steps and trailed after Tom. Inside the office with the door closed, Tom held out the note.

Brett glanced at it and laughed.

'Bet this throwed a scare into Lawrence. That guy jumps every time the wind changes.'

'Told him to print it,' Tom said.

'What?'

Anger flashed in Brett's face.

'The Deeds is behind this. You gonna let them put a threat like that in the paper?'

'Town's got to know what it's up against,' Tom said.

'You're wrong,' Brett said. 'The Deeds boys want publicity. Want people to think they're something. Want folks to be scared of them.' Brett stared at the star on Tom's waistcoat. 'You've given them just what they want.'

'They want a reckoning,' Tom said. 'Says so right here.'

Brett glared at him.

'We should get up a posse right now. Hunt 'em down like dogs.'

'We don't know where to look. Anyway, slipping a note under a door ain't a crime. Best wait and see what they intend to do next.'

'Folks in this town reckon you're a brave man,' Brett snarled. 'How are you gonna follow Tom's footsteps?' they ask me. Well, I know different. If you was such a hero you'd be saddled up right now. Of course they wrote the note. Who else would have written it?'

'Maybe so,' Tom agreed. 'But I tell you one thing. I'm a lawman, not a hero. If you want to enforce the law, you don't go riding around with some bloodthirsty posse at your heels.'

'Unless we go after these Deeds boys they're gonna come after us,' Brett said. 'This is a fine mess you've left me with.'

Brett started to pace up and down the office. His boot heels hammered the cottonwood floor.

'Tomorrow morning, when I'm sheriff, I'll be raising a posse,' Brett went on. 'I'll expect every young, able-bodied man who can shoot to ride with me.'

'Note was pushed under the *Herald*'s door last night,' Tom said. 'Where were you last night?'

'What?' Brett flared. 'You saying I engineered this? You reckon I want to pick a fight with the Deeds?'

'Never said that,' Tom said coldly.

'I was in town,' Brett snapped. 'You saw me.'

'Stay late?'

'What do you want to know for? I was in the saloon for a couple of hours after we put Jeb Deeds on the train. I was last to leave.'

Tom nodded.

'Reckon it's a good thing you're quitting,' Brett said. 'Never heard such fool questions.'

He waved dismissively at Tom, flung open the door and strode out.

* * *

Soon after midday everyone assembled in the saloon. Swaths of red and white bunting hung round the walls and across the ceiling. Above the bar were more paper rosettes. The place was packed; the rows of seats which faced the bar were filled and a standing crowd crammed in at the back of the room. Mayor Brogan sat at a table up front with his committee, Bill Gifford and Doc Andrews. At the side of the room Tom and Brett waited to be called.

As the hands on the clock over the bar rose to twelve, Brogan got to his feet. Everyone fell silent as he skated through the preliminaries, how pleased he was to be here, how El Cobarde had grown and prospered over the past decade and a half, and how certain people had led the community with unswerving dedication. Then he got on to the main business. He called Tom to stand beside him and shook his hand. Most of all, he said, the town owed a debt of gratitude to one man, the one man who had earned the respect of them all, who had kept the streets safe and who had brought criminals to justice. He presented Tom with a half-hunter engraved on the back with his name and the dates of his office.

Tom accepted the watch and handed Brogan his sheriff's star in exchange. He added a few modest words about finishing his house because fifteen years was just too long to see the stars every night, and everyone laughed. He went on to mention by name folks he had daily dealings with in the town and recalled some of the amusing things which had happened: the day Doc Andrews's horse wandered in to the sheriff's office and ate a mouthful of papers off the desk; the time a snake-oil salesman passed through, selling his patent hair restorer which turned out to be root ginger and axle grease, and all the bald fellas walked around for a week with their heads caked in it. There were more stories; people applauded with unmistakable warmth.

Mayor Brogan turned to his son. Brett brushed aside his father's platitudes about hopes for the future, snatched the sheriff's star from his hand and announced that the town was in danger. Cold silence sliced through the good-humoured conversation. Brett told the story of the letter which had been pushed under the door of the newspaper office and how they would all be able to read it in the next edition of the *Herald*.

'You'll see what we're up against,' Brett said. 'That's why I aim to raise a posse. I want any man brave enough to face down the Deeds to ride with me.'

He glanced at Tom who was watching

from the edge of the room.

'We don't know where they are,' Tom interrupted. 'A posse could ride for days, search every cave in the Trans Pecos and still not find them.'

'You saying we do nothing?'

Brett's question hung in the air. The room waited.

'I'm asking how we can find them if we don't know where they are,' Tom said.

Mayor Brogan interrupted. 'Brett's sheriff from now on in. If he wants a posse . . . '

'There'd be no one left to defend the town,' Tom said.

A buzz of conversation rose. People in the crowd searched the faces of Brett and Tom. Brett reminded them of those young officers they had come across in the war whose untried self-belief staked everything on a daredevil chance of success; Tom's experience advocated calm and caution.

'That's right,' Brett snapped. 'I'm sheriff now. If it was up to me all the

Deeds boys would be in jail. Tom Rider only did half a job. He put Jeb away for a few years but he didn't catch his brothers.'

'What about Ellie?' someone called from the back of the room.

Brett exploded. 'Who said that?'

'I did.' It was Eli Feather, who worked at the grocery. 'I only meant she might have an idea where the Deeds boys are holed up.'

'She don't,' Brett snarled. 'She ain't seen none of her family since her ma died and that was years ago.'

'I'm declaring this meeting ended,' Mayor Brogan said suddenly. 'If the new sheriff wants to summon up a posse, that's up to him. In the meantime, I know you folks are ready to set up trestles outside for all that home-cooked food you've brought along. I suggest you all move your chairs outside and come up to the bar if you want to. We'll be eating shortly. Let's all remember this is our send-off for Tom. Any other business can wait.'

The atmosphere relaxed as the audience got to its feet. Bill Gifford and Doc Andrews waved Tom over.

People avoided catching Brett's eye. For a moment he felt alone and believed everyone was turning away from him. He was sheriff now. They should listen to him. He rounded on his father.

'Why did you break up the meeting? I hadn't finished.'

'You want people to agree with you, you've got to make them think it's their own idea,' Brogan hissed. 'Everyone respects Tom. If he's disagreeing with you, you've lost.'

'I'm sheriff,' Brett countered.

'You are,' Brogan said under his breath. 'And you've got a lot to learn.'

It didn't take long before the food was ready. Trestles lined the street laden with cold cuts, whole roast chickens, fresh-baked cornbread and apple and apricot pies. Brett fixed a smile on his face and nodded to people he knew in the crowd. Some of the men touched their hats to him and one or two called him Sheriff. He relaxed. Tom and Mayor Brogan had stayed inside the saloon and, without them looking over his shoulder, he was able to come into his own.

Eli Feather fetched his fiddle and began to scrape out a few reels. At the sound of the lively tunes laughter quickened the conversation. Unable to keep still, some of the young guys started to move their feet. People complained about the dust they kicked up and, still playing, Feather led them away from the tables of food out into the middle of the street where his bow swooped and dived over the strings and the music picked up speed.

Men brought jugs of beer down the saloon steps; soon laughter rose in the sunlit afternoon. Tom and Mayor Brogan came out onto the porch, with Brogan trying to persuade Tom to exchange his lemon water for a whiskey.

The two men reminded each other what a desolate piece of land this place had been ten years before. As they congratulated themselves once again on what they had achieved, they noted a dust cloud which marked the progress of a lone rider approaching from the direction of the railhead. They weren't expecting anyone and the rider was making speed.

When the rider got closer Tom recognized William Lever, a railroad clerk.

Feather put aside his fiddle and the dancers turned to gape as Lever's horse pounded up the dusty street. Catching sight of Tom outside the saloon, Lever leapt down from the saddle and ran up the steps. He waved a brown envelope.

'Wire just came through,' he gasped.

He thrust the envelope into Tom's hands. Before Tom could open it, Brett leapt up the steps two at a time.

'I'm sheriff now.'

He snatched the envelope and ripped it open.

'It's from the prison governor.'

Every face was turned towards him.

REGRET TO INFORM. MIDNIGHT TRAIN HELD UP AT CUTTER'S ROCK. PRISONER 0255 JEB DEEDS ESCAPED. NUMBER CASUALTIES UNKNOWN AT PRESENT TIME.

3

Brett Brogan turned on his father.

'Believe me now?' he snarled.

The mayor took a pace backwards; his son's anger unnerved him. Everyone was watching.

'Got to get Jeb Deeds before he gets to us.' Brett's call was a rallying cry.

He paced the saloon porch, holding the wire high above his head.

'Which of you is going to step up? Which of you is going to ride with me?'

'If you wait, Brett — ' Tom began.

'Wait?' Brett laughed.

'We know they're coming, all we've got to do is be ready,' Tom said.

Brett turned to the crowd.

'Hear this? Hear what our former sheriff is saying?'

People shook their heads, not yet convinced.

'The Deeds family has been a thorn

in the side of this town for years,' Brett shouted. 'The sheriff should have dealt with them a long time ago.'

Johnny Gifford, Bill's son, stepped forward. He wore new ranch clothes, polished boots and a red neckerchief that he had put on for the dance.

'Obvious, ain't it?' He appealed to the crowd. 'We got a new sheriff now and he's got to clear up a mess left by the old one.' Then he added, 'I say it's time for the young men to decide what's to be done.'

There were catcalls in the crowd then. The young men laughed out loud at this outrage.

'Now listen,' Mayor Brogan thundered. This debate was getting out of hand. 'We've got to be careful here. What happens if a posse rides out of town and the Deeds brothers show up while they're gone?'

'That's what I've said all along,' Tom added.

'Jeb Deeds was convicted of rustling my longhorns in the first place,' Bill

Gifford said. 'If my men ride off in a posse, his brothers could cut the herd again.'

A division formed in the crowd. The young wanted action, the older men spoke up for caution. Voices were raised as people started to argue. Some of the women supported their sons, others sided with their husbands.

Then Brett's voice broke over everyone.

'I'm sheriff and I aim to hunt down Jeb Deeds and his brothers. Any man brave enough to ride with me, meet me here at first light.' He caught Tom's eye. 'I guess that means the young fellas. The old guys better stay and look after the town.'

There was general murmuring in the crowd: it seemed a fair compromise. But the spirit had gone out of the party now. Tables laden with food were untouched; the jugs of beer were full.

'C'mon, Eli,' Brett called over the heads of the crowd. 'Play us a tune.'

'Play all night if folks want to dance,'

Eli called back. 'But before I do, I want you to know that I'm with Tom Rider. Tom's been a friend of mine for a long time. I played for the dance at his wedding. Last summer when that twister blew the roof off the store, Tom was the first one to come and help with the repairs. Can't believe he ain't going to be sheriff no more.'

Eli was getting dewy eyed. Brett glared at him.

'Wouldn't take you with us anyway, old man.' He looked around to see who was listening. 'What could you do if you came up against Jeb Deeds — fiddle him to death?'

A few of the younger guys applauded.

Brett marched down the steps, poured a glass of beer and strode over to where the dancers waited. He kicked out a few steps in the dust until Eli fell in with him and the music started again. The dancers came to life. By the start of the next tune, couples were waltzing under the afternoon sun.

Conversation picked up and people

moved back towards the tables of food. Brett raised his glass to his father who stood with Tom on the saloon porch. A self-satisfied grin was slapped on his face.

William Lever turned to the mayor.

'What shall I tell them at the depot?'

'Tell them what you heard. A posse rides at dawn,' Brogan said. 'You got weapons down there?'

'There's a shotgun on the office wall,' Lever said.

'Any dynamite left?' Tom said.

'There's a box in the safe,' Lever said. 'No one's touched it since the tracks were laid.'

Tom considered.

'Just tell the sheriff before you go.'

Lever headed down the steps.

As Tom, Brogan and Bill Gifford stepped back inside the saloon, the party came to life. Eli's fiddle scraped and skirled and the volume of talk and laughter intensified round the food tables.

'Too hot for us old guys out there,'

Bill Gifford said. 'We got to sit in the shade.'

The others laughed.

'Used to love dances when I was a young man,' Bill continued. 'Met my Annie at a dance.' He smiled to himself. 'That was in the days when there would be a fiddle player in every house, sometimes a guitar player too. Saturday nights, they'd all come together and we'd dance till sunup. Now all we got is old Eli scratching away.'

The others laughed.

'I never was one for dancing,' Tom said. 'Elizabeth used to say she'd walk to a dance and limp home afterwards.'

'Never mind the dancing,' Brogan said. 'Hope these young fellas don't drink too much if they're intending to ride out in the morning.'

Tom considered. 'Still say they're wasting their time.'

'We're outvoted,' Gifford said grimly. 'If Johnny is going to ride out with the posse, guess I'd best head home and look out my Winchester.'

'I'll head out to my place,' Tom said.

'Stay in town with me,' Brogan said. 'No need for you to go out to that old half-built house.'

Tom laughed. 'This is my new life. Got to make a start on it sometime.'

Outside, Eli's music jumped and swooped. More dancers joined in. From the sound of the whoops and laughter, the beer jugs were emptying fast.

Tom got to his feet. Bill Gifford followed.

'If anything happens here,' Brogan said. 'I'll send word.'

* * *

Tom rode out of town as afternoon subsided into evening. The land was flat here all the way to the riverbank where Tom's house stood. A pair of pronghorns leapt ahead of him over a carpet of lacy switchgrass. Patches of dropseed pushed through buffalo grass and glowed yellow in the late afternoon sun; the skyline was broken by stands of

55

scrub oak and necklace trees.

A mile further on, the roof of Tom's house came into view and beyond it the tops of the screw beans and walnuts that lined the riverbank. The next few months' work lay ahead of him. He had put it off for so long now, the loose shingles and the half-completed porch seemed normal. He intended to finish the construction, cut back the greenery and sell up; completing the house would close the chapter he had opened with Elizabeth. His first job would be to uproot the dead magnolias she had planted on either side of the porch steps. They had never taken.

After settling his horse in the barn Tom climbed the porch steps and entered the house. There were three rooms, each facing the river. Everything was dusty and neglected and the place smelled of dry rot. Frail grey cobwebs linked the chairs to the table; sand had blown in and covered the floor. A mouse skittered away as he entered the bedroom. Tom unbuckled his gunbelt, hung it by the kitchen door and threw all the windows wide. Mesquites had grown up during the summer and blocked the view of the river.

Finding a broom in one of the cupboards, Tom swept the kitchen. He cleared the old ash from the stove and lit it. Soon the place was filled with the friendly smell of woodsmoke and coffee. He ate some of the corn bread and chicken he had brought with him from the party and carried his cup of coffee down to the river in the dying light.

Tom found his favourite spot and leaned back against a walnut trunk. The last of the sunlight reflected pink and gold on the slow water. Fireflies dodged and darted over the surface and somewhere by the opposite bank a fish plopped. Reeds moving in the breeze sounded like rice spilling on a table top. Tom reached in his pocket for his tobacco and rolled a cigarette. He took a deep draw and let the peace of the evening soak into him.

This place had everything Tom had once wanted: the tranquillity isolation brings, the calm of being beside the river. He could have loved it here. His parcel of land ran along the bank, wide enough to keep a milk herd or carry a corn crop. He knew Bill Gifford would sell him extra acreage at a knock-down price if he wanted to expand. At one time that would have been his plan.

But tragedy struck. Before Tom had the chance to complete the house, Elizabeth died; the reasons he had to live out here died with her.

With a generosity that Tom never forgot, Brogan arranged for him to lodge rent-free and all-found at the saloon; Tom transported the timber he had been going to use on the house back into town to build the sheriff's office. He threw himself into his work. He got into the habit of coming out here once or twice a month to tend Elizabeth's grave under the sycamores and keep an eye on the place. He couldn't find it in his heart to continue with the construction.

The peace and calm which had drawn Tom to this riverside spot had turned into cold loneliness. But he was determined. Elizabeth had loved it here. She would have wanted him to finish the house and would have been dismayed by the state he had let it fall into. Thomas took one last pull on his cigarette and flicked the glowing end into the river.

At first Tom thought he was mistaken. Then he was sure. Hoofbeats from the direction of town. Two horses? Three? The horses were still a mile away but riding hard. His mind raced. Jeb Deeds and his brothers? Who else could it be?

Tom hurried back inside and buckled on his gunbelt. He paused to blow the dust off the oil lamp that stood on the kitchen table and light it. Then he hurried out to the stable, slung the saddle on his horse and led him outside. The hoofbeats were louder now.

As he pulled the horse deep into the shadows and looped the reins round the branch of a mesquite, Tom heard the first shot. The horse shifted uneasily and stamped his foot. Tom blew into his ear and smoothed his neck.

Treading lightly round the side of the barn, Tom positioned himself where he had a good view of the yard, the porch steps and the door to the house. Light from the oil lamp glowed through the window and round the edge of the door where it had warped in last winter's rains. It was hard to tell but the hoofbeats seemed to be further away now. As he crouched down pain lanced through his knees.

Clouds slid apart and moonlight bathed the plain. The rye grass was silver and the leaves of the mesquites looked cast in steel. Tom couldn't tell whether the riders were far away now or had stopped altogether. Then a shadowy figure slipped across the yard and hid in the darkness under the porch.

'Thomas,' the man hissed. 'You in there?'

Thomas slid his .45 out of its holster.

'Tom, it's me, Eli.'

Before Thomas could answer, Eli climbed up onto the porch and was silhouetted against the lamplight.

'Tom, you in there?'

A rifle shot cracked and the bullet sang through the air. Eli threw himself down.

'By the barn,' Tom hissed. 'Keep low.'

He heard Eli crawling over the loose boards of the porch. Another rifle shot cracked. The bullet tore through the branches of the mesquites. Then Eli emerged, crawling on his belly in a pool of moonlight, and hauled himself alongside Tom.

'Jeb Deeds chased me out of town,' Eli gasped. 'Had his brothers with him. They had sticks of dynamite, threw 'em every which way. There ain't much left of the sheriff's office, I can tell you that.'

Eli paused to get his breath back.

'They were calling out your name. Asking where you were.'

'Didn't anybody get a shot at them?' Tom said.

'It happened real fast,' Eli said. 'One minute everyone was dancing a polka, the next the sheriff's office was raining down on top of us. No one was wearing sidearms because of the dancing. By the time they'd all run to fetch 'em the Deeds boys was gone.'

'Did Brett get up a posse?'

'They were arguing about that when I left: whether it was better to ride after 'em in the dark or wait till first light. I headed out to warn you. Cut through on the lower road.'

Tom scanned the flat land. The desert grass and the few trees were lit in pale monochrome light.

'They followed me,' Eli said. 'I dismounted and let old Whiskey run on to try and fool 'em. He'll have doubled back to town. That may have bought us some time.'

'Good of you, Eli,' Tom said.

A cloud moved across the moon; darkness curtained the plain.

'You can see that lamp from a mile away,' Eli said. 'If they come to the house, we'll have a clear view of 'em.'

'Reckon Jeb Deeds has already figured that out or they'd be here by now,' Tom said.

As he spoke there was a crack as someone trod on a dry stick somewhere in the undergrowth behind them.

4

Tom and Eli crouched tight to the barn wall and stared into the darkness. Tom eased back the hammer of his Colt. Away to the right the oil lamp glowed through the window of the house; the orange light fell on the porch and the yard. The whisper of the reeds on the riverbank was faint; an owl's scream pierced the night somewhere far away. Something shifted in the undergrowth close to them.

Without warning a cloud slid aside and uncovered the moon; the yard and the house were washed in silver light. A horse stood at the edge of the brush, its reins trailing the ground.

'Whiskey.' Eli scrambled to his feet. 'He followed me.'

He smoothed Whiskey's neck and his flank. The gelding nickered and ducked his head in pleasure.

'We should take it in turns to get some shut-eye and head into town at first light,' Tom said.

* * *

Grey light weakened the darkness in the east as Tom and Eli set out. They followed the line of trees along the river for a while, then turned abruptly along the dirt track to the town.

Outside the saloon the posse was mounted up. Brett was at the centre, explaining the route they were to follow. His voice was urgent and excited. Ellie Deeds was beside him on a young appaloosa. Her dark hair was scraped back under her hat; her beautiful face was sullen and angry. Brett stopped talking when Tom and Eli rode up.

'Well, look who it is.'

Tom greeted him. The guys in the posse turned.

'Come to join us?' Johnny Gifford called.

'Too late,' Brett said quickly. 'We're

ready to ride. No more room in this posse.'

'Which way are you headed?' Tom asked.

'Right to where the Deeds boys is at,' Brett crowed triumphantly. 'Persuaded Ellie to show us their old haunts. They'll be in jail by sundown.'

In the east the sky was blood red.

'They chased Eli Feather out towards the river last night,' Tom said. 'After they paid a visit here.'

Brett glared. 'I know what you're thinking. We should have chased 'em out of town right then. Well, we couldn't. They surprised us.'

'I wasn't thinking that,' Tom said.

He tightened his grip on the reins.

'They won't get away,' Brett said. 'You can be sure of that. Not with Ellie showing us where they'll be.'

Brett turned to Ellie for agreement but she looked away from him. He clicked his tongue and his horse moved forward. Ellie and the others followed. They rode past the sheriff's ruined office and out of town.

Tom and Eli dismounted and crossed the street to what was left of the office. The window and part of the front wall had been blown out; the door and a section of the roof was missing. Splintered cottonwood planks, shattered glass and the broken door lay in the street. Inside, the desk was upturned, the record books were scattered everywhere and the cell door swung open.

'He's leaving it like this?' Eli said softly.

Mayor Brogan called to them from the saloon porch.

'Reckon Deeds thought you were in there.'

He gestured them to follow him into the saloon.

Inside, the row of oil lamps glowed above the bar. Brogan took a seat at a table overlooking the street. Tom and Eli joined him. A barkeep cleared away the posse's breakfast plates.

'Brett's taken Ellie with him.' Tom

shook his head. 'Shouldn't have done that.'

Brogan shrugged.

'It's hard enough for that girl with the way Brett is,' Tom went on. 'Now he's expecting her to hunt down her own brothers.'

'Reckon she'll do it?' Brogan said.

Tom noticed the way Brogan failed to meet his gaze.

'She's a good kid,' Tom said. 'What chance did she have?'

In the east, red dawn pushed across the sky.

'She's leading them into the desert,' Eli said. 'Gonna be mighty hot out there today.'

'If they do find Deeds, the weather's gonna be the least of their problems,' Tom said. 'How's Jeb Deeds going to react when he sees Brett's brought Ellie with him?'

He stared across the street at the sheriff's wrecked office.

'Jeb Deeds is too smart to be caught a second time,' Tom said. 'I reckon he'll head back here to finish what he started.'

★ ★ ★

Tom and Eli headed out to the railhead and left Brogan to supervise clearing the damage. They were fearful about what they would find. William Lever, his clerk and the shotgun they kept on the wall would have been no match for the Deeds brothers. William Lever came out of the office with a shotgun in his hands as soon as he heard their horses.

'Sure am glad to see you fellas,' Lever said. His shirt was torn and blood-spattered; a purple bruise twisted his mouth.

'When I tried to stop 'em taking the telegraph machine, they knocked one of my teeth out.' He sounded more indignant than hurt. 'Took the dynamite out of the safe, too.'

Lever threw down the shotgun. 'Don't know why I'm holding this thing. They took my box of shells.'

'You on your own out here?' Tom said.

'Clerk took off at the gallop as soon as Deeds showed up.'

'You stayed?'

'Took my horse,' Lever said. 'Left me a canteen of fresh water and that's all.'

'Guess you'd better come into town with us,' Tom said. 'Best if we all stick together.'

'No can do,' Lever said. 'A hundred head due here from Bill Gifford's place within the hour. Train's due to collect 'em this afternoon.'

'And Jeb Deeds is out there some-where with nothing to lose and sticks of dynamite in his saddle-bags,' Eli said.

'And I ain't got a telegraph machine to warn Kansas. What am I supposed to do when Gifford's boys turn up with two hundred head — tell 'em to turn round and go home?'

'Maybe they won't come,' Tom said. 'Bill knows the Deeds are on the loose.'

'They'll come all right,' Lever said.

'Gifford ain't missed a shipment since the railhead opened. He's got buyers all lined up.'

Tom and Eli dismounted.

'Guess we better wait with you.'

'Where's the new sheriff?' Lever asked. 'Why ain't he here?'

'Got up a posse at first light,' Eli told him. 'Took Ellie Deeds with him. Reckons she'll show him some of the places Jeb might be holed up.'

'Took him on a wild-goose chase, more like,' Lever said.

'Got a screw of coffee in my saddle-bag,' Tom said. 'Stove lit?'

Lever nodded.

The wooden hut set back from the railway track doubled as Lever's place of work and living-quarters. Papers were everywhere and wires lay across the desk where the telegraph machine had sat. Lever's bed was upended; feathers from his pillow settled over everything like snow. Tom made a pot of coffee and set it on the stove.

'Did they give any sign of what they

were going to do?' Tom called. 'Or where they were headed?'

Lever righted a chair and sat down.

'Nope. There was just a lot of whoopin' and hollerin'. Reckon if I'd have objected any more they'd have put a slug in me.'

'One of us could ride up the line,' Eli suggested. 'Flag the train down.'

'If Jeb Deeds has got the same idea you'd run right into him.'

The air juddered; the unmistakable thud of an explosive charge followed. A flock of whimbrels flurried into the air somewhere down near the river. Their high, whistling cries warned of danger.

'What's he doing?' Lever wondered. 'Dynamiting fish?'

The men looked at each other. They waited for a second charge but it didn't come.

'Posse will have heard that,' Lever said. 'They'll know where Deeds is.'

'They could be miles away,' Eli said.

Lever scanned the horizon.

'See that?'

A white dust cloud billowed up into the air five miles south.

'Bill Gifford's longhorns,' Lever said. 'Got to get the pens open or they'll wander all over the line. Johnny Gifford gets real mad if the pens ain't open. He likes to drive the cattle right in.'

'Won't be riding with 'em today,' Tom said. 'He's out with the posse.'

'This is the last year for longhorns,' Lever continued. 'Johnny reckons he's gonna cross 'em up with some English breed so the steers'll carry more meat.'

'Been longhorns on the Gifford place since anyone can remember,' Eli said. 'My pa used to cowboy out there. Turned to store-keeping when his horse threw him.'

The men watched the dust cloud move in the bright morning air.

'Johnny says longhorns were good in the days when whole herds had to be taken on drives. They're tough. Don't need much water. Those days are gone now. Now there's more profit in a cross where the beeves are heavier.'

Tom had been listening while he watched the cloud.

'What does Bill Gifford say?'

'Never heard him speak on it,' Lever said. 'Johnny calls his pa stuck in his ways and a whole lot more besides.' He laughed. 'Reckons his pa is the last rancher in the whole of Texas to carry longhorns.'

'Sure will be a shame if they disappear,' Eli said. 'A few years ago folks would have said Texas without longhorns ain't Texas.'

The cloud was moving nearer. The men could just make out the rumble of hoofs on the hard ground.

Lever walked down to the cattle pens and began tying back the gates. Eli and Tom picked up papers and righted the furniture in the railroad office.

'Reckon we should stay here in case the Deeds boys show?' Eli asked.

'They'll know Gifford's men will be here for the loading,' Tom replied. 'If they're intending to rustle the steers, my guess is they'll stop the train further up the line.'

'If?' Eli laughed. 'Jeb Deeds is a rustler. What else is he going to do? Way he thinks, these steers is just waiting to be took.'

Tom leaned back against the wall of the railroad office and watched the shifting white cloud. As it shrank and swelled against the blue sky, dust particles sparkled in the sunlight. Seen from here it looked like a jewelled, luxurious thing rather than a choking cloud of dirt kicked up from the ground which filled the mouths and stung the eyes of the men and animals that made it. He felt for his pouch of Bull Durham and rolled a cigarette.

'Don't reckon Jeb Deeds is interested in rustling today,' Tom said. 'Don't reckon he'll be coming here at all.'

Eli looked at him.

'That dynamite charge,' Tom said. 'Only one place that could have come from.'

'I know,' Eli said.

'That was my house by the river. Jeb Deeds knew I wasn't there. He was sending me a message.' Tom stared over to where the whimbrels had risen into the sky. 'When I head back into town, reckon he'll be waiting for me.'

In the south, the dust cloud levelled as Gifford's men slowed the herd for the last half-mile. Tom and Eli could make out the animals now, flowing like a brown river over the dusty plain. The cow punchers wheeled round the herd, leading, cajoling and keeping the steers tight together for the entry into the stockyard. As they drew closer, Tom and Eli could hear their calls and whistles above the rumble of hoofs.

* * *

The dust cloud enveloped the railhead like fog. Dust settled on the roof and obscured the windows of the wooden office. It matted the manes and invaded the coats of the horses. It covered the clothes of the men, got in their eyes and

76

choked their throats. Tom and Eli watched the cowboys guide the steers into the pens, eyes screwed up, kerchiefs over their faces. Lever hurried back and forth between the pump and the troughs with brimming buckets of water in each hand.

'Why don't you let me ride on ahead?' Eli suggested. 'Jeb Deeds won't harm me. If I spot him I could send you a signal.'

'Jeb Deeds is smart,' Tom said. 'If he's in town, someone will have told him where we are. If he sees you on your own, he'll know what we're playing at.'

Tom clicked his tongue and his horse moved forward. Eli followed. Outside the dust cloud the bright sun and the clear air was a relief.

The town lay ahead of them, a collection of sun-bleached wooden buildings on a vast empty plain. Away to the west the river was hidden from view and along the horizon the peaks of the Trans Pecos were visible through the haze. A family of jack rabbits watched them pass from under the shade of a box tree. The sound of lowing cattle and the shouts of the hands receded behind them.

'I'm asking you one more time,' Eli said. 'Jeb Deeds ain't got no quarrel with me. Let me ride on in. If I see anything, I'll fire a shot in the air.'

Tom didn't smile this time. 'Wait here, Eli. This is between me and Jeb Deeds.'

Tom spurred his horse. Before Eli had time to reply, it leapt forward and soon powered onward at a gallop. Eli stared after his friend.

Tom rode hard to the edge of town. The horse's mane lashed the air; his hoofbeats thundered. Tom felt the massive strength of the animal under him; the air stung his eyes; he tasted salt on his lips. Tom's senses were alive.

People said Tom was a brave man, and he enjoyed his reputation. But this was what he always did: he headed straight towards danger so he did not have time for fear. Right now the only thing in his mind was where the first shot might come from. His eyes fixed on the roofline where someone with a Winchester might be waiting.

The buildings on the edge of town flashed past. Tom raced along the street and reined in his horse when he reached the square. Innocent bunting waved in the breeze; the banner with his name on it hung overhead. The trestles had been cleared away and had left a patch in the middle of the street where the dancers had stamped the dirt down hard.

Tom wheeled his horse around. Where was everybody? Usually there would be men on the saloon porch, women outside the store, riders on the street. Tom scanned the rooftops again, took in the first-floor windows and paid attention to the shadowy alleys between the buildings. There was no one.

Riding slowly across the square, Tom kept the reins loose in one hand while the other rested on the handle of his

.45. The place was a ghost town. Opposite the saloon an empty cart leaned on its shafts. There was nobody on the porches or at the windows. Doors were all closed even though the heat of the day was rising fast. Blinds were drawn across the window to the newspaper office and the livery stable door carried a chain and padlock.

In front of the saloon Tom jerked the reins and stopped dead. His blood froze; his heart smashed in his chest. In an untidy pile, just where a cart had unloaded them, were three pine coffins. Beside them, slung down in the dirt were three coils of rope; the end of each one was wound into a noose.

5

As Tom rode up to the coffins he could see that there was a word gouged on the end of each one. He glanced back over his shoulder. The square was empty; there was no sound from any of the buildings. He checked along the roof-tops where a shooter might hide, unholstered his .45 and slipped out of the saddle.

A sudden movement made him start. A black vulture made a clumsy landing on the other side of the square. It folded away its white-tipped wings as though it was putting its hands in its pockets, and stared at him.

Still holding on to the saddle, Tom stooped to peer at the word cut into the ends of the pine boxes. Names. 'Gifford' was nearest. The middle box said 'Brogan'. Tom knew the name on the third coffin before he read it. He looked closely to be sure. 'Rider', in clumsy letters.

Ice-water ran in Tom's veins now. He was aware of the easy balance of the .45 in his hand. His mind was sharp as it always was when he faced physical danger. He scanned the rooftops and registered the upper windows once more. No one. He hauled himself into his saddle.

Traces of dust lifted a little from the square as a warm wind blew in from the desert. A coil of tumbleweed rolled ahead of Tom's horse. The town which only yesterday was full of prosperity and bustle had had the life terrified out of it. The wooden buildings stood silent as tombs. Tom half-wished he had let Eli Feather ride in with him.

Someone called Tom's name. The word played on the breeze. Then a face appeared in a window above the saloon. Mayor Brogan.

'Up here, Tom.'

The face ducked back out of sight.

Tom dismounted and looped his

reins round the rail in front of the saloon as casually as he had a thousand times before. His horse dipped his head to drink at the water trough. There was one on each of the four sides of the square.

With his .45 ready in his hand, Tom mounted the steps. Inside the saloon, it took a moment for his eyes to adjust. In the shadows he saw upturned tables, chairs slung aside and a carpet of broken glass on the floor. An oil lamp lay on the bar. The glass shade was smashed; oil leaked over the polished wood and dripped onto the floor.

Brogan appeared at the top of the stairs. His face was bloody and swollen. He waved a Winchester dangerously.

'Thought you were dead,' he hissed. 'Get up here.'

Upstairs, Brogan had barricaded himself into a bedroom with a view of the street. He heaved a wardrobe across the door as soon as they were inside. There was a loaf of bread, a canteen and a box of shells on the bed. Brogan immediately took a seat at one side of the window and nursed his Winchester.

'They came in after the posse left this morning,' Brogan said. 'A whole army of 'em.'

'How many?'

'Twenty. Maybe more. Jeb Deeds broke into the jail and freed the prisoners. Prison governor didn't send a wire,' Brogan said. 'Didn't have any warning.'

Words tumbled out of him as he kept his eyes on the street.

'Posse wasn't here. All the young guys had gone with it. You weren't here. Bill Gifford's men were out cowboying. There was only me, Doc Andrews, the women and children and a few old-timers. No match for twenty guys.'

Tom nodded.

'Jeb Deeds stood on a cart right there where everyone was dancing yesterday. He said anyone who didn't want to watch me hang should clear out right then and there.'

Brogan's grip tightened on the Winchester.

'Everyone high-tailed it. Even Doc.'

'Why did they let you go?'

Brogan turned to him. One side of his face was a mass of bruises.

'Bait. They said if I was here, you'd come looking for me. Soon as they let me go, I grabbed the Winchester that's always kept under the bar downstairs and holed up here. What else could I do?'

'You could have run like the others.'

'Think they'd left me a horse?'

'We could make a run for it right now,' Tom said. 'What's to stop us? Two of us could ride my horse.'

'They're out there,' Brogan said. 'You didn't see 'em but they watched you ride in. Sure ain't gonna let you ride out.'

Tom peered out of the window. Nothing. Just the vulture waiting in the empty square.

'You sure?'

'Some of 'em are in the room over

the hardware store,' Brogan said. 'Don't know where the others are.'

'You know why he's doing this?'

'When Jeb Deeds was standing on the cart he started shouting that it was time this town had real justice. How it was time for a reckoning. No one was listening much by then. The guys who had broken out of jail were smashing up the saloon and helping themselves to what they wanted from the store. They were waving sticks of dynamite. Everyone grabbed what they could carry and high-tailed it as quick as they could.'

'Real justice?' Tom said.

Brogan went back to keeping watch at the window.

'That's what he said.'

Tom considered. 'Know whose names are on those coffins down there?'

'Jeb Deeds wrote 'em on with me watching,' Brogan said.

He sat down on the bed and stared out of the window. In the far distance above the roofline, the Trans Pecos were misty blue in the sunshine. A mile to the west, silver dust hung in the air over the railhead. Nothing moved. The midday heat held everything still.

'Bill built that ranch with his own hands,' Brogan said. 'When he'd finished building that he lent his men to build the town.'

Tom scanned the street.

'We both worked hard,' Brogan continued. 'Petitioned the railway company to build the line down here. That wasn't no small thing. All we wanted was to make life better. All that was here before me and Bill came was dirt and buffalo grass.'

One of Brogan's eyes was swollen shut.

'We did it together,' he went on. 'Took you on as sheriff and built a place honest folks can be proud of. Now we're ready to pass it on to the next generation and this happens.'

'I don't get it,' Tom said. 'Justice for what? Jeb was tried before a judge and jury.'

'Wouldn't be paradise without a

snake,' Brogan said grimly. 'The Deeds have been snakes around here for a long time. The only peaceful time we had was when those boys were too young to bother anybody. The minute they grew, they were trouble.'

'If Hank Deeds had managed to get his hands on a piece of land so his sons could grow up on their own farm, it might all have been different,' Tom said.

The train had pulled in to the railhead. In the distance, fists of white smoke punched through the heat haze.

Brogan rounded on him.

'You taking their side?'

'I'm saying if Hank Deeds had had his own place it would have given his boys something to work for,' Tom said. 'Might have kept them out of trouble.'

'Hank Deeds was never any good. You know that.'

Warning blasts from a steam whistle sounded in the distance.

'Ellie tried her best but those boys went feral,' Brogan went on.

'They never had nothing,' Tom said.

'How did you expect 'em to turn out?'

There was blood on Brogan's lips.

'Hank Deeds shot your wife,' Brogan said. 'You trying to make excuses for him?'

Tom stared out into the empty square.

'What happened happened,' Tom said. 'I've had ten years to ponder it. Now I reckon those Deeds boys suffered as much as anyone. Even as much as me.'

Brogan took a slug of water from the canteen and flung it down on the bed.

'That's all in the past,' he said. 'Right now we've got to figure out how to get out of here.'

Judging by the column of smoke, the train was on the move. They could follow its progress through the railhead dust and out into the clear air of the desert. Sunlight flashed on steel. Clearly visible was the engine reversing up the line, shunting the cattle trucks ahead of it.

There was a sound downstairs.

Someone was in the saloon below. Tom and Brogan froze. Both men silently reached for their guns.

There was a footstep on the stairs. Tom cast his eye over the wardrobe Brogan had dragged across the door. How long could that protect them?

Turning to scan the street through the window, Tom caught Brogan's eye. Brogan was like an old bull pawing the ground, holding on to his fury until it was time to charge.

They listened hard. More movement below. Someone was walking backwards and forwards across the bar. Was he looking for something? Brogan and Tom stared at each other.

Then there was the tapping of a hammer from the bottom of the stairs. Tom listened for a second, then heaved the wardrobe aside with a crash and threw open the door. A clatter below. Boot heels hurried over the broken glass. Brogan turned to the window with his Winchester at his shoulder.

Tom was out in the corridor now. He

inched his way along the wall, his .45 in his hand. He paused at the corner to the stairs.

There was a shout from Brogan.

'Couldn't get a clear shot. He's slipped around the side.'

Keeping low, Tom spun round the corner and aimed his .45 down the stairs. No one. And no sound from the saloon. He took each stair carefully, paused to listen after every footstep.

Something caught Tom's eye. A note was tacked to the newel at the bottom of the stairs. A discarded claw hammer lay beneath it.

Tom snatched the note with his left hand while covering the saloon with his .45 with his right.

Brogan called out again.

'Anything?'

'No.'

Tom backed up the stairs, keeping his gun ready.

Upstairs, Brogan guarded the window.

'Slipped round the side of the building,' he explained. 'Kept so tight to the wall I couldn't get a clear shot.'

'Look at this,' Tom said. He threw the note down on the bed.

Brogan reached across, glanced at the note, crumpled it in his hand and threw it down. He turned back to the window.

'Reckon they'll try to rush us?' Brogan said.

'They're waiting for something,' Tom said. 'Or they would have done that already.'

'What?' Brogan snapped. 'I'm getting sick of this. That young hoodlum is playing us like fish.'

Tom fell silent for a while. Then he said, 'Maybe they want to keep us pinned down till the posse gets back.'

Brogan laughed. 'I'm hoping the posse will get back. I brought Brett up to be a fighter,' he said. 'Brett and Johnny Gifford will see Deeds off.'

'Maybe he needs an audience.'

'For what?'

'Aims to hang us,' Tom said. 'What good's a hanging unless there's someone there to watch?'

'That's crazy,' Brogan said. 'Don't make sense.'

But he fell silent. He stared out of the window. His knuckles were white on the stock of his Winchester.

'Four hours till dusk,' Tom said. 'If they don't come for us, maybe we can get up on the roof and slip out that way.'

Brogan nodded.

The note lay on the floor between them where Brogan had thrown it. The yellow paper was crumpled into a ball. There, in awkward capitals, were four words. HAVE YOUR CONFESSIONS READY.

6

'What does it mean, 'Have your confessions ready'?' Brogan spat. 'What confessions?'

'Deeds got something against you that I don't know about?' Tom asked.

Brogan stared out of the window. Dust lifted in the breeze; a ball of tumbleweed chased across in front of the buildings.

'Jeb Deeds appointed himself judge and jury now?' Brogan said. 'Who does he think he is?'

'I arrested him fair and square,' Tom said. 'Caught him out in the desert with a hundred head of Bill Gifford's longhorns and the irons ready to change their brands.'

'This ain't about rustling a few steers,' Brogan said.

'Reckon this has got something to do with the way Hank Deeds died?' Tom asked.

'That was years ago,' Brogan snapped. 'What are you saying?'

'Jeb was there. You forgetting that?' Tom said.

'He was just a kid. Anyway, he ran off. It was dark. He didn't see nothing.'

'Always said he did,' Tom said.

'He took his pa's side,' Brogan snapped. 'What do you expect?'

Brogan turned back to the window again. The tumbleweed hesitated.

For a while, neither man spoke. Brogan concentrated on the view from the window; Tom moved a chair so he could cover the door. As the hottest point of the day passed, a wind got up. It moaned through the empty buildings like a lament.

* * *

Tom had known Jeb Deeds since he was nine years old. Back then he'd been a moody scrap of a kid with the bad temper that comes of growing up hungry. Ellie, his older sister, kept house and brought up him and his brothers as best she could in a shack on Bill Gifford's ranch.

Hank Deeds worked as a stockman for Gifford. As he was faced with bringing up four children on his own, Gifford let him have the use of an old bunkhouse. The place hadn't been used since Gifford acquired land on the other side of the ranch that was better grazing, and the hands moved over there. Gifford's idea was that while carrying on with his job as a stockman, Deeds could keep a milker and some hogs as well as having somewhere for his children to live.

At first things went well. Deeds moved himself and his kids into the building and made a few alterations to make the place habitable. He bought a piglet, built a pen and ploughed a patch of land for corn.

In those days children were used to hunger, but on stockman's wages Hank Deeds was barely able to provide for them. If young Ellie hadn't been a scrupulous housekeeper, they would have starved.

Bill Gifford told everyone he had done the right thing. He had gone out of his way to help one of his men who had hit hard times; he had waived payment and did not expect any rent. What more could he do? As his ranch grew and prospered, he raised the wages of the workers. Hank Deeds benefited from this too.

After a year or two, it was clear that Jeb and his brothers were growing up wild. Their father worked long days on the ranch and while Ellie did her best to keep the boys fed and clothed, they began to get into trouble. They developed a reputation for being brazen and untrustworthy; the towns-folk believed they would steal anything they could. They were banned from the store; as sheriff, Tom was frequently called on to halt their intimidating behaviour. People disliked them on sight.

It could have been the strain of

being unable to control his unruly sons; it could have been some form of revenge against the townsfolk who were contemptuous of him and his brood; it could just have been a desperate attempt to lever himself out of poverty. But within a few months of Tom being appointed sheriff, Hank Deeds attempted to steal twenty head of Bill Gifford's longhorns. Tom raised a posse and went after him.

There were only two places to which he could be headed: Preacher's Crossing or Anvil Pass. Preacher's was the next station up the line, where he could load the cattle onto trucks which would take them north to Kansas; Anvil was a steep-sided gulch in the southern Trans Pecos on the route the cattle drives had followed before the railroad was built. Tom caught up with Hank Deeds twenty miles out in the desert one June Sunday morning after trailing him for two days.

Deeds gave himself up without protest. He had taken a wrong turn in the desert and the steers were half-dead with thirst. It was almost as if Deeds wanted to be caught because he knew his plan, if you could call it a plan, was doomed from the start. Tom escorted him into town while Gifford's men drove the steers back to the ranch.

Tom didn't have the heart to lock Hank Deeds up. His children's lives were already impossible; without him, how would they survive?

Tom hadn't reckoned on the anger of the townsfolk. The loathing for the Deeds clan was widespread. Now it erupted. The urchin children were reviled and their father was beneath contempt. Townsfolk petitioned Tom, demanding Deeds be denied bail; people called on Bill Gifford to throw him off his land; an anonymous letter appeared in the *Herald* which called for rustlers to be strung up like they were in the old days.

Tom let Deeds return home but warned him that if public pressure persisted, next time the judge passed through he would have to stand trial. Tom told Deeds to go back to work, keep his children away from the town and lie low. The furore died down; months passed without incident.

It wasn't until an announcement appeared in the *Herald* that Judge Emerson would be passing through on a sweep of the courtrooms in the eastern part of the state, that folks remembered Hank Deeds and his disastrous attempt at cattle-rustling. Tom and Mayor Brogan rode out to Gifford's place and had a sit-down with Bill, where they decided what to do.

Because of the number of times he had been called to the saloon to deal with their drunken father, Tom had always been sympathetic to the Deeds children. Brogan and Gifford were not normally known for their tolerance of ne'er-do-wells, so Tom was surprised at the leniency they were prepared to extend to Hank.

In order to pacify the restive elements in the town, the three of them came up with a plan. Tom would make sure Hank Deeds attended court; Brogan and Bill Gifford would put in a plea for clemency; Hank Deeds would give a good account of himself. Judge Emerson would see that the sheriff, the mayor and the accused's employer had the matter in hand and would let him off with a warning.

Angry letters appeared in the newspaper again as the trial approached. Vilification of Deeds and his children became the currency of street-corner gossip. But Tom was confident he had the matter in hand. Brogan's and Gifford's testimony would ensure the judgment they wanted; the fact that Deeds was up before the court would satisfy the townsfolk that justice would be done. The judge would come and go, Deeds would be reprimanded and life would return to normal.

One other thing happened that caused tongues to wag. Two years ago Brett Brogan, the mayor's son, was first seen walking out with Ellie Deeds. They were a handsome pair. Ellie was nineteen. She was no longer the skinny kid who struggled to keep house for her father and look after her wayward brothers, she was beautiful. Her long black hair was swept back from her forehead, her intelligent eyes sparkled and her honey skin glowed over perfect cheekbones.

Brett had grown into a rangy, muscular young man, sandy-haired and square-jawed. His height gave him a commanding presence; being the mayor's son lent him supreme confidence. Some folks said he was arrogant. With his deputy's star pinned to his shirt and Ellie Deeds on his arm he strode through the town like a prince.

Of course, the town gossips pursued the couple with relish. While they were forced to admit that these two were probably the best-looking couple south of the Trans Pecos, Ellie Deeds became the object of their disdain. How dare she presume to walk out with the mayor's son? All the Deeds were untrustworthy, why should she be any different? She was a gold-digger. It was obvious she was trying to get her claws into Brett because she knew that one day he would be sheriff. How could a respectable town have a sheriff who was connected to a family of lawbreakers like the Deeds?

* * *

Colours deepened in the empty square. Shadows filled the spaces between the buildings. The warm breeze which had blown in from the desert most of the afternoon cooled by a degree or two.

There was a shout from one of the buildings. Brogan tightened his grip on the Winchester. Tom joined him at the window.

'You two ready to confess?'

The voice was light and casual. It was a young man's voice, mocking them.

'Jeb, is that you?' Tom called.

Brogan raised the Winchester to his shoulder and squinted down the sights.

'You ain't answered my question.'

The tone was matter of fact, as if it was explaining something obvious that they had failed to grasp.

'He ain't gonna show himself,' Brogan muttered. 'Ain't got the nerve.'

'Reckon I'll have to leave you a while longer,' the voice called again. 'Reckon you ain't ready yet.'

Brogan lowered his rifle.

'We don't know what you're talking about,' Brogan hollered. His exasperation showed through.

'Yes you do. Especially you, Brogan. I was there too, remember.'

Brogan turned to Tom.

'What's he talking about?' he hissed.

Tom shook his head.

'We don't know what you're talking about,' Tom shouted.

There was silence after that. Just silence, as if there was no one there and there had never been a conversation.

'Jeb?' Tom called.

No answer.

'Jeb Deeds, I know you can hear me.'

No answer.

'This is Tom. Come on now, Jeb.'

Tumbleweed rolled round the empty square. Evening shadows were dark between the buildings.

'Don't reckon he can hear me,' Tom said. 'Maybe he's took off somewhere.'

'You gonna set foot outside the door? You'll find out that way,' Brogan said.

Tom considered. Then he stood up and holstered his gun.

'Cover me.'

Brogan listened to Tom's footsteps echo on the stairs. He heard them crunch on the broken glass on the saloon floor below. He made out the creak of the hinges as Tom pushed the saloon door. Then he heard the young man's voice again.

'Come out to make your confession, Tom?'

Brogan couldn't tell whether or not Tom could see who was addressing him. Then he heard Tom's voice.

'If you've got something on your

mind, Jeb, you better spit it out right now.'

'You're a brave man, Tom, standing there talking that way. I got you covered. I just got to squeeze my trigger finger and you'll be dead.'

Brogan raised his rifle and scanned the windows opposite. They were as dark as the shadows between the buildings. Jeb could be behind any of them.

'Your meaning ain't clear, Jeb,' Tom said. 'That's what I'm saying.'

'Best get back inside, Tom. Talk to Mayor Brogan. Maybe he understands better than you do.'

'Posse will be coming back soon, Jeb,' Tom said. 'You thought of that?'

A rifle shot cracked and the bullet bit the saloon wall close to Tom's head. Tom flinched.

'Inside now, Tom. I ain't gonna say it a second time.'

Back in the upstairs room, Tom turned to Brogan.

'He seems to think you know more

about this than I do.'

'See anybody?' Brogan said. 'How many of 'em are there?'

Tom took a swig of water from the canteen and threw it back on the bed.

'Could be Jeb Deeds on his own, for all I know,' Tom said.

'It'll be dark in a couple of hours,' Brogan said. 'We got a chance then.'

'Posse might be back before that,' Tom said.

Brogan settled down by the window again and nursed his Winchester.

'Sure there's nothing you want to tell me?' Tom said.

Brogan stared at him. 'You believe this nonsense about confessions? Jeb Deeds is a lowlife. He was born one and he stayed one.'

'He's clear about what he wants,' Tom said.

'And what's that?'

'Wants me to talk to you because he says you understand what this is about better than I do.'

'Just watch the door,' Brogan

snapped. 'I'll stay watching the window.'

Light faded from the room. Outside, shadows spread across the square. Whether Brogan knew anything or not, Tom couldn't tell. He was used to the mayor's irritable manner. Everyone knew Brogan didn't suffer fools.

Just as darkness was complete, Brogan slowly lifted his Winchester to his shoulder. Hoofbeats sounded in the square.

'Wait,' Tom hissed.

He joined Brogan at the window.

'It's Brett,' Brogan said. There was delight in his voice. 'Told you it would be the posse.'

'Brett,' Brogan called. 'We're up here. Above the saloon.'

A pistol shot cracked. Wood splintered on the window frame. Brogan ducked back into the room.

There was more movement out in the square. There was the murmur of men's voices, hoofbeats and the whinny of horses. Brogan and Tom tried to make out what was going on but the darkness was like a closed door.

'Reckon we should try for the livery stable,' Brogan said. 'While they're occupied.'

The men slipped across the room and down the stairs. Their hearts exploded at each creak of the old cottonwood boards. They picked their way over the glass on the saloon floor. They edged round the table in the storeroom at the back of the bar and felt for the door.

Tom's hand rested on the handle. He stood, waited and listened. He heard three things: a mouse skittering across the floor, his heart crashing against his ribs and Brogan's tight, anxious breathing.

As Tom turned the handle the iron key, which had rested in the lock, clattered to the floor. The sound seemed to echo round the town. Everyone must have heard it. Tom froze. Then he tried again.

The handle turned. Tom inched the

door open. A draught of cool air touched his face. The hinges creaked and the key scraped on the floorboards. He froze again. Every fibre of him strained to hear a sound outside. Nothing. Just the faint rustle of the breeze in the mesquites. He pulled the door open. Night air washed over him.

A voice said 'Come to make your confession?'

They heard the snick of the hammer of a .45 being drawn back. Tom hurled himself back into the room, cannoned into Brogan, felled him like a tree and kicked the door closed. Shots from a pistol bit the door. They both scrambled back, crashed into the table and through the door into the saloon.

On the other side of the building someone had lit torches in the square. Tom and Brogan edged forward. The broken glass snapped under their feet. Torches were in their iron holders on the wall of the store opposite the saloon. Their orange flames reared into the night.

Tom looked closer. There was someone tied to one of the pillars. A man's
body was slumped forward, supported
by ropes round his chest. Unconscious,
or in pain? Tom couldn't tell. As they
watched, he raised his head. His face
was bloody; he grimaced at the
tightness of the ropes. At first neither
Tom nor Brogan recognized him. It was
a fair distance across the square; it was
dark; bruises disfigured the man's face.
Then he called out. Strain frayed his
voice as if the effort was too much.

'Tom, you in there?'

It was Bill Gifford.

7

'Tom?'

The word clawed in Gifford's throat.

Staying back in the shadows of the wrecked saloon, Tom drew his .45 and kept his eyes on the square. Gifford raised his head and stared into the darkened building.

'You in there, Tom?'

There were men in the shadows a few yards on either side of where Gifford was tied, just outside the flickering torchlight. Above them, clouds shielded the moon.

'Could blast 'em.'

Brogan's hoarse whisper came from the darkness on the other side of the saloon. The barrel of his Winchester protruded from the shadows.

'One of us has got to get up on the roof,' Tom said.

'You crazy?' Brogan hissed.

'Can you think of another way out?'

Brogan was silent.

'Tom?'

Gifford's voice again. Torchlight danced on his bruised face.

'Talk to him,' Tom hissed. 'And keep talking.'

As Brogan called out, Tom edged back across the saloon, trying to avoid the glass. The darkness seemed to amplify every creak of the cottonwood boards.

'It's me,' Brogan shouted. 'You hurt bad?'

Tom did not wait for the answer. At the turn in the stairs he strained to listen, but Gifford's voice was weak and too far away.

On the landing, Tom fetched a chair from the bedroom and stood it under the trapdoor which gave access to the space beneath the pitch of the roof. His shoulders burned as he hauled himself up. How long did he have before Deeds realized he was not down in the saloon with Brogan?

Once up in the loft space, Tom stooped low and placed his feet on the joists. The darkness disorientated him; the air smelled dry and cushioned him with warmth. Silence beat in his ears like wings.

When Tom came to the end wall, he felt around for the door that led into the roof space of the adjoining store. He scrambled through. His back ached from being bent double; his hands were bruised from knocking against the roof timbers. At the far end, he paused again and listened.

Nothing. Just the soft crash of his own heartbeat in the darkness.

Tom ran his hands over the shingles above him. One of them must be loose. Splinters tore his fingers and made him gasp with pain. He tried row after row. Every one was nailed down tight. His shoulders burned from twisting in the confined space; his back ached from being stooped for so long. His mouth tasted of dust.

Then he felt something. A blade of

night air crossed his face.

Tom craned around, searching for the gap in the shingles. He reached out to grab a joist to support himself but the joist wasn't there and he fell in a crashing explosion of lath and plaster, through the ceiling into the room below.

A pile of buckets broke his fall and scattered like clanging bells as his shoulder bit the wooden floor. He was in a storeroom for the hardware store. Tom lay still with buckets rolling over him and waited for the cacophony to stop. Someone must have heard. Tom picked himself up. Nails of pain drove into his knees; his back and shoulders were alight.

The storeroom window overlooked the square. Light from the torches burned a hole in the darkness. Bill Gifford hung forward against the rope as if he was too weak to stand. He struggled to keep his head upright. Why wasn't Brogan talking to him? From here, Tom could make out the figures of men keeping back out of the flickering torchlight. There were four of them, maybe more, close to the edge of the shadows. Then there was Brogan's voice.

'Bill, you OK?'

No answer. Gifford's head was bowed. The ropes took his weight.

'Talk to me, Bill.'

Gifford raised himself up slowly as if it cost him all his strength. His voice broke. 'They aim to kill us. There ain't no way out this time.'

'Shut up, Bill. Don't say that.'

Then Brogan shouted, 'Hey, Jeb Deeds. You out there? I don't know what you think you're playing at.'

Someone called back. A young man's voice from the shadows. 'You do. You know what I'm playing at.' He laughed. 'I've told you. I want your confession, Brogan. You and the others. Then I'm going to hang you.'

'You're crazy,' Brogan said. 'Confession to what?'

'You need to think harder, Brogan.'

Deeds's voice mocked him. 'Tell Tom Rider he should be thinking on it too.'

A rifle shot cracked then. And another. Brogan had had enough. The men who had been standing at the edge of the torchlight dived for the shadows. The Deeds twins, Luke and William, were amongst them. The yellow flames showed Gifford's terrified face. Tom waited for them to return Brogan's fire but none of them did.

'There's your confession,' Brogan yelled.

The words hung in the air after the sound of the shots died.

Gifford flinched. Someone standing close to him struck a match. The end of a stogie fizzed in the darkness. The ratchet sound of Brogan cocking his Winchester carried across the square. It wasn't a stogie. A spluttering flame arced in the darkness; something bumped on the saloon porch and rolled into the doorway.

In a split second, Brogan yelled, then the yellow flash of a dynamite explosion lit everything; an earthquake roar followed. The walls of the saloon buckled outwards with the force of the blast; Brogan was pitched head first through the window; the doors were flung wide and the ground shook.

On the other side of the square the image of half a dozen men was frozen in the sudden flash. Jeb Deeds and his two brothers stood in front of them with .45s strapped to their hips. The men cowered behind them, unarmed and in torn prison-issue shirts.

Deeds drew his gun and gestured to the men. Tom saw them launch themselves towards the saloon. He heard their feet stampede over the hard earth and Brogan's muffled cries as they fell on him.

Jeb shouted something; the group of men dragged Brogan into the pool of torchlight and dropped him in the dirt. The Deeds brothers pushed the men aside, hauled Brogan upright and lashed him to the pillar opposite Bill Gifford. His head lolled forward as the ropes took his weight.

'Brogan?' Gifford said. His voice was weary.

Brogan didn't answer.

Tom backed away from the window. How long before they realized he wasn't in the saloon? He holstered his gun and stepped carefully between the buckets. There was another window in the corridor behind the room. There were sounds next door now. Footsteps on the wooden boards. Men's voices. They were searching for him.

Tom levered the window open. The sash rattled and announced to the world where he was and what he was about to do. Boot heels stamped on the staircase next door. Was someone outside waiting for him?

With his gun in his hand, Tom climbed through the window and jumped. He landed on his feet. White blades of pain shoved into his knees; for a long moment agony arced through him. He tumbled forward. He tore his shirt at the shoulder and the dirt on his face became mixed with blood. He lay still and waited for the shock of the fall to retreat out of him.

Tom could hear the men calling out to each other in the saloon. Someone had fetched a torch. He saw the orange light cut between the planks of the back wall. They were shouting now. No caution any more. They had searched the building and knew he wasn't there. He heard someone shouting from the roof space. They had found the open trapdoor.

The .45 was comfortable in his hand. Tom pushed himself to his feet. He staggered out into the darkness away from the buildings. A few yards further he found a tree trunk and slumped against it. He could hear the men's footsteps rattle along the floorboards inside. The orange glow of the torches in the square rose above the roofline.

'Who's that?' There was a voice somewhere out in the darkness.

Tom thumbed back the hammer on his .45.

'Tom, is that you? This is Eli. Don't shoot.'

Cautious footsteps.

'Keep your voice down,' Tom hissed.

Eli felt his way towards him.

'What's going on?'

Deeds's men called out to each other in the buildings, confident now because there was no one there. A torch appeared at the window; two faces peered blindly into the darkness.

'How many are there?' Eli said. Fear grazed his voice.

'Enough,' Tom said. 'They got Brogan and Bill Gifford.'

'They got the mayor?' Eli echoed. 'Didn't anybody try to stop them?'

'They're planning a necktie party. Want me to join 'em.'

Eli whimpered. 'Where is everyone?'

'Posse's still out searching. Rest of the town's run off.'

'Everyone?'

'Deeds didn't give 'em a whole lot of choice.'

The moon slid out from behind a

cloud. The wooden back walls of buildings, the shingle roofs and the open window through which Tom had jumped were lit in silver. The ground where they were crouched was scattered with sagebrush and mesquites and soon ran into open desert.

'We gonna wait for the posse?' Eli asked.

Tom hesitated. 'If the posse ain't here by now, I reckon it ain't coming.'

'What?'

'Ellie Brogan is leading 'em round the old caves where the Deeds used to hole up. Reckon she'll keep 'em out of town till Jeb sends her a signal.'

'I could high-tail it out to Gifford's place,' Eli said. 'The cow hands would help.'

'Only old-timers left,' Tom said. 'The young fellas have rode with the posse.'

'What choice do we have?'

'All right,' Tom said. 'Make sure you let everyone know what they're in for.'

Eli got to his feet. 'Figured out why they're doing this?'

'Jeb Deeds has got some kind of a grudge,' Tom said.

As a cloud curtained the moon, Eli waved to Tom and hurried into the shadows. Tom rested the .45 on his knee. The buildings were quiet now. The men seemed to have headed back to the square. The glow from the torches made a silhouette of the roofline.

Tom hauled himself to his feet. Burning wires threaded through his knee joints; every step was agony. He moved to the back wall of the store, felt his way along and turned down the alley between the buildings.

The men walked about openly in the square now; some of them held bottles of red-eye. Jeb Deeds and his brothers were hunkered down on the saloon steps.

Across the square, Brogan and Gifford were still tied. Under the torchlight, terror shone in their faces. Every now and then, one of the men in ragged prison clothes would walk up to

Brogan and feign a punch which just stopped short of his belly or missed his jaw by a fraction. Sometimes they would sling some insult in his face or scream a question which he could not answer. When they tired of tormenting Brogan, they crossed over and tried to get a reaction from Bill Gifford.

'You the sheriff?' one of them shouted. 'You're the sheriff, ain't you?'

Bill's terrified denials didn't cut any ice.

'Yes, you are. You're lying, ain't you?'

It was a game. The more they played, the more they enjoyed it. The more unnerved their victims became, the more the men laughed.

Deeds and his brothers kept their distance. A whiskey bottle from the saloon sat beside them on the step but they weren't drinking. They rested their feet on a case of dynamite and kept an eye on the men enjoying their new-found freedom. They were the only ones who were armed.

Tom hung back in the shadows and

kept his eyes on Jeb. Was this how Jeb had looked all those years ago when he was hiding out in the darkness? Jeb had been an unsmiling kid then; he was stony-faced now.

Why had Jeb come back? Tom wondered. There was nothing for him to come back to. His folks were dead, his brothers were set on their careers as lawbreakers, Ellie was stepping out with Brett Brogan. The shack where he had grown up had collapsed through neglect.

Then as now, Jeb had sat in the shadows and watched everything. As a boy, his sullen face masked a quick temper; now it disguised contempt for a cruel world that had treated him harshly. He watched the men torment Brogan and Bill Gifford and was indifferent to it. Smiles passed across the faces of his brothers as they watched; Jeb remained stone.

A pistol shot cut through the night. Deeds and his brothers jumped to their feet. Brogan and Gifford raised their heads. The men in the square stood still. Everyone waited for a second shot. Jeb Deeds drew his gun and stared into the darkness beyond the edge of the square.

Maybe a lookout had got jumpy. Some animal had probably ventured close to the buildings.

Then there was a disturbance some-where beyond the buildings. Hoofbeats. Shouts. Jeb Deeds's hand went to his gun again. There was another shot. Riders were approaching.

Tom hung back. The alley gave him a good view of the square and provided the cover of shadows.

There was a warning shout.

'Comin' in. Don't shoot.'

Jeb Deeds hollered a reply. The men who had been tormenting Gifford and Deeds melted into the shadows.

Two horsemen rode in. They wore the same ragged prison clothes as the others. A man stumbled awkwardly between the two horses. His arms were roped to his sides by the lassos held tight by the riders. He fought to keep his balance. If he stumbled, they dragged him through the dirt until he managed to pick himself up onto his feet again. His face was bruised, his coat was dusty and torn. The holster on his hip was empty; one of the riders held up a trophy .45.

As the riders dragged their prisoner into the circle of torchlight, Tom caught his breath. It was Eli.

8

Jeb Deeds unholstered his gun and strolled across the square. He jabbed the barrel up under Eli's chin and hissed questions at him; torchlight dappled Eli's terrified face. Quick to lose patience, Jeb raised his arm and slammed his pistol down across the back of Eli's skull. His legs buckled and he slumped forward. Jeb nodded to the riders; they released Eli from the ropes and let him crash to the ground.

Eli's horse must be somewhere, Tom thought. Could he find it and ride for help? Just as the idea settled in his mind, Tom knew it was no good. Jeb was set on catching him. Look at Brogan and Gifford, they were half-dead already. Thoughts buzzed in Tom's brain like flies caught behind a window.

Jeb moved himself to a corner of the saloon porch away from the others. He let his brothers watch over the men in the square while he set a torch burning in the iron stand by the saloon doorway. He carried the pile of notebooks from the sheriff's office with him, righted a chair and settled down to read.

From where he hid, Tom could see that the covers had faded; these notebooks dated back years. What had caught Jeb's interest?

As darkness weakened in the east, the men in prison clothes bedded down on porches round the square. Some of them scoured the buildings for blankets, others lay down where they stood. Brogan and Gifford leaned back against the wooden pillars and closed their eyes. The Deeds boys rescued chairs from the saloon and sat with their feet up and their pistols ready while they snatched some shut-eye. Jeb Deeds read on, book after book.

Jeb was looking for something. He flicked through the pages of a notebook until some sentence caught his eye. Sometimes he ran his finger down a page before he started to read. If he didn't notice anything, he threw the book aside and grabbed the next one. When something interested him, he read intently.

In the past, Tom reflected, Mayor Brogan had teased him about the painstaking way he had recorded the sheriff's business. 'Whoever's gonna read it?' Brogan would laugh as he tried to persuade Tom to abandon his desk and join him in the saloon. Here was his answer.

Grey light spread across the sky and everything was still until a black vulture landed in the middle of the square with a squawk and a flurry of feathers. It folded its wings, stood still and jabbed its head from side to side to get its bearings. It sized up the men tied to the posts and made a few tentative hops in the direction of Eli's body sprawled in the dirt.

One of the men in prison clothes noticed. He threw a stone which landed a foot short of the bird and made it jump backwards. A second made it unfold its wings and lever itself up into the air. The bird found a vantage point on the roof of the grocery store from where it could watch and bide its time.

Tom settled himself down in the alley to wait. He would have to confront Jeb, he knew that. With daylight cleaning the sky, it was just a question of when. Should he wait for the posse? Should he surprise Jeb now while his men were asleep? Thoughts twisted in Tom's brain. He looked at Brogan and Gifford with their hands tied behind them and blood on their shirts. Would Jeb listen to anything he had to say?

*   *   *

Far away but unmistakable, the sound of hoofbeats woke everyone. The men on the porches sat up. The Deeds brothers pushed their hats off their faces and swung their legs to the ground. Jeb looked up from the journal he was reading. Brogan and Gifford raised their heads.

Sunrise bled into the eastern sky and made a red wound along the horizon. The men around the square settled to wait; the Deeds brothers checked their Colts. Unconcerned, Jeb went back to his reading.

The thunder of the hoofs of a dozen horses entered the far side of town. They slowed as they reached the square and arrived in a billowing cloud of dust. Ellie was on her horse out front; the other horses were riderless and roped comfortably together by their bridles. The end of the rope was looped round Ellie's saddle.

Jeb stepped down from the porch of the saloon and waved a greeting. His brothers hurried over to her.

'You did it,' Jeb shouted.

Ellie slipped out of her saddle. The Deeds boys moved forward to take care of the horses.

'They need feed and water,' Ellie said. 'It's been a hard ride.'

She patted her own horse on the

neck and smoothed his mane. This was Starlight, the beautiful appaloosa Ellie had cared for, whispered and raised from a foal. He turned and nuzzled into Ellie's shoulder.

While his brothers led the horses to the livery stable, Jeb crossed the square and kissed his sister. He was delighted to see her. Then he noticed something, smoothed the hair away from her face and stared at a bruise on her cheek. His face fell.

'Don't say anything about that,' Ellie said. 'I handled it.'

She held up her palm to warn him to back off. Jeb scowled.

'Plan worked,' he said. 'Where did you leave 'em?'

'Camped out by the spring at Hammer Ridge.'

'Twenty miles,' Jeb said. 'They'll be here by nightfall.'

'It was easy,' Ellie said. 'Those guys sleep like the dead. Rode across Mesquite Flats right up to the caves at Pinetop yesterday then cut back to the

Hammer. Wore 'em right out.'

Ellie flashed a smile.

' 'Course, they wasn't expecting me to take off with the horses in the middle of the night, so they didn't set a guard.'

'Best get you some breakfast,' Jeb said.

'Long as you don't expect me to cook it. That pig Brogan insisted I cook chow for the whole posse last night even after I'd been scouting for 'em all day.'

She looked Jeb hard in the eye.

'I mean it. I kept house for pa and you three for years. I can outride and outshoot the whole bunch of you and you still expect me to do the cooking.'

'Not me.' Jeb raised his hands in mock surrender. 'I don't expect nothing.'

' 'Course you don't, little brother.'

Daylight filled the square now. The men had led the horses away. Ellie held on to Starlight's reins. She and Jeb started to walk back to the saloon.

'Let one of the guys take care of

Starlight,' Jeb said.

Ellie looked doubtful. 'I normally see to him myself.'

She took a Winchester out of the saddle holster. 'You need a rest,' Jeb said, and waved one of the men over.

Ellie kept her eyes away from Gifford and Mayor Brogan as she and Jeb crossed the square to the saloon.

'One missing?' she said.

'Don't worry,' Jeb said. 'We'll find him.'

As they turned to climb the saloon steps, Mayor Brogan called out.

'Can't you do something, Ellie?' His voice cracked with despair. 'You ain't going to leave me like this?'

Ellie turned to Jeb. 'Confessed yet?'

Jeb shook his head.

'I'm reckoning to be your father-in-law,' Brogan whined. 'I made Brett sheriff. What are you doing this for?'

Ellie looked at Jeb again. 'Ain't he figured it?'

Jeb shrugged.

'Mayor Brogan.' Ellie turned square

135

to him. 'You know what your son did a while back?'

Brogan looked confused.

'He took my Winchester away and hid it. Told me I wouldn't need it now I was with him because shooting wasn't womanly.'

'Well, Ellie, I'm sure Brett — ' Brogan began.

'I'm sure Brett knew I was a better shot than he was,' Ellie interrupted. 'Just like everyone else did. Think that had anything to do with it?'

'Brett wasn't a bad shot, Ellie. You've got to allow that.'

'Couple of nights ago he brought out my Winchester from wherever he'd hidden it and used it to shoot my dog. Got anything to say about that?'

'The dog bit him, Ellie. If a dog ain't been trained not to bite then he has to be put down,' Brogan said. 'It's kinder in the long run.'

Ellie's voice hardened. 'Seeing as you weren't there, you won't know that the dog was defending me. Brett comes in at two in the morning because he's been celebrating after putting my brother on the prison train.' Ellie paused to let her story sink in. 'He starts shouting about this and that and how there ain't no food ready for him. He kicked Ranger and when Ranger thought he was going after me he tried to stop him.'

'If he bit someone, Brett was in the right. You got to see that.'

For a second, Ellie thought Jeb was going to lunge at Brogan. She grabbed his arm.

Brogan sensed he had gone too far. 'He gave you your Winchester back,' he said. 'I can see that.' He attempted a smile.

'You're an arrogant man, Brogan,' Ellie said. 'You brung up your boy the same.'

'My son is sheriff,' Brogan sneered. 'When this is over, he'll be running this town. If it wasn't for him you'd be living in a one-room shack ducking and diving from the law like your no-good brothers.'

Ellie tightened her grip on Jeb's arm.

'He didn't give me anything back,' she said. 'He brought my Winchester with him yesterday. Wouldn't give it to me last night so I took it.'

'Well,' Brogan said. 'That's probably — '

'Had to shoot him, though.'

'What?' Brogan screamed.

'A scratch,' Ellie said. 'You know how good a shot I am. Could have made it a whole lot worse.'

Brogan gaped.

'After that I gave him the whiskey bottle and he slept like a baby.'

Ellie held up the Winchester as proof.

'You Deeds. Your pa was no good. None of you are.' Brogan was beside himself. 'I warned Brett about stepping out with you but he wouldn't listen.'

Jeb leaned over to him and prodded him in the chest. 'Enough.'

Fear flickered in Brogan's eyes.

'Next time you open your trap,' Jeb said. 'I want to hear a confession.'

On the way up the steps to the

saloon, Jeb turned to Ellie. 'Why did you walk out with Brett? None of us ever understood that.'

Ellie sighed wearily. 'He was the best-looking guy I'd ever seen. I didn't care that he was going to be sheriff. I didn't care what he was going to be. I just didn't want to open my eyes one morning and wake up next to some pork belly.'

Jeb laughed.

'Because you ain't a woman, you won't properly understand what I'm talking about.'

The smell of frying beef filled the saloon. Ellie helped Jeb right a table and found chairs for them both. She made him set them close to the broken window so they could keep a check on Brogan and Gifford.

*   *   *

Tom hung back in the alley round the corner, close enough to earwig what Jeb and Ellie said. He heard Jeb tell her he had read the record books.

'It's all in there,' Jeb said. 'Now I got it figured out.'

'Lucky I taught you to read,' Ellie said.

Jeb started to tell her what the sheriff's record said about the night their father died. Tom heard the clatter of their cutlery on the saloon's china plates; Ellie did not interrupt while Jeb told the story.

Having seen to the horses, the men filed into the saloon in search of breakfast. If Jeb and Ellie were still talking, their conversation was drowned out. They had to be planning something. If Tom hung tight and found out what it was, there was a chance he might be able to get the upper hand. He checked his Colt. Better bide his time.

A short while later Tom heard Jeb and Ellie on the porch. Their voices were low and he couldn't make out what they said. They seemed to have come to some sort of decision.

Then someone rapped on a table and called for silence.

'I want to thank you for staying with us this far,' Jeb announced. 'The posse will be back by nightfall and they ain't going to be in a friendly mood after walking all day.'

He paused to let their laughter and catcalls die away.

'What I'm saying is, we've got some family business to take care of. If you leave now, you'll have a full day's start on the posse.'

'We can't outrun them, boss,' someone shouted. 'Even if we start out now they'll catch us tomorrow.'

'Not if you take their horses.'

Silence.

'You're giving us the horses?' The voice was incredulous.

Then Ellie spoke. 'They had a long ride yesterday and they kept going most of the night too. You'll have to rest them. An hour's ride, an hour's rest.'

There was a murmur of agreement.

'If you keep that up all day you could

be at the border soon after dark if you head south. If you're heading north, you'll be somewhere near Hammer Ridge.'

There was a storm of conversation.

'On top of that,' Jeb crowed, 'the posse won't have any horses to chase you with.'

'Don't you want us to stay and help you?' someone said. 'You busted us out. We owe you a debt.'

'You've done enough. Throwed a scare into the town and showed 'em we mean business. What we got to do next is family.'

'Posse gets back, you'll be outgunned,' someone shouted. 'Ain't you thought of that?'

'I've thought of it,' Jeb said. 'But like I said, this is family business.'

The men began to pour out of the saloon. Barefoot, dressed in prison rags, pale and malnourished, they were happy as bees. As the sun rose they made their way round to the livery stable.

Luke and William Deeds said their goodbyes to Jeb and Ellie. They had decided to take their chances and head south. They said some of the banks in the small towns were practically unguarded; the men they had freed from jail looked up to them now and had offered to show them easy routes to slip backwards and forwards across the border. Ellie didn't try to stop them.

Tom pressed himself to the saloon wall to keep out of sight. He knew what Jeb and Ellie wanted now: a reckoning for their pa.

* * *

Eight years ago. The night Hank Deeds died had been the worst night of Tom's life. Once he'd written everything up in the sheriff's record he'd tried to bury the memory of it so deep it could never be dug up again. Of course, he hadn't been able to. What happened had haunted him day and night ever since.

That night Tom's life as well as the

Deeds kids' had changed for ever. What could Jeb and Ellie hope to gain by unearthing everything? Jeb had been a ten-year-old kid at the time, who didn't know what he saw; Ellie hadn't been there anyway.

One thing was clear. Jeb and Ellie blamed Brogan, Bill Gifford and Tom himself. Still Tom didn't get it. Weren't they the ones who had helped them after the catastrophe happened?

Tom had always felt sorry for Hank Deeds's children. He had spoken up for them when others railed against their wild ways. Despite the terrible thing their pa had done, he, Tom, had looked out for them. Never for one second had he blamed them. Now he doubted everything. If this was the way they repaid him maybe he had been wrong. Maybe they were treacherous and feral like the townsfolk said.

Cold anger filled Tom. Did Jeb really intend to pin the blame on him as well as Brogan and Gifford for his pa's death? Hank Deeds had been an incompetent rustler and a drunk whose children grew up wild. He was the man who had come out to Tom's half-built house one night all those years ago and right there in front of witnesses shot Elizabeth, Tom's darling wife, stone dead.

9

'Anything in the books?' Ellie said.

She and Jeb were back on the saloon porch now. The men had filed round to the livery stable.

'Everything,' Jeb said. 'If one of his prisoners sneezed Tom kept a record of it.'

Overhearing his name, Tom tightened his grip on his Colt.

'He believed everything Brogan and Gifford told him. Wrote it down in black and white,' Jeb went on. 'And that's what he told the judge.'

'No one to contradict him,' Ellie said. 'What do you expect?'

'Is he a good man or a liar?' Jeb said. 'I've been around liars so long, I can't tell any more.'

'He trusts people,' Ellie said. 'That means he believes what they tell him. And that don't do no one any good.'

146

Jeb chewed on that for a moment. 'You're saying it takes a bad man to do good?'

'That's about it,' Ellie said.

Jeb laughed to himself. 'Sounds just like us.'

The first of the riders wheeled round the corner from the livery stable and came to a halt in front of the saloon. He had made a rope bridle and rode bareback. The morning breeze caught his ragged prison shirt. New-found freedom had put a glint in his eye. Others drew up beside him.

'Want to thank you, Jeb.'

Jeb held up his hand modestly.

'Needed you to help me,' Jeb said. 'Had to bust you out of jail first.'

'Most of these guys ended up behind bars because they were poor,' the man said. 'Or they took the fall for some fella who was smarter than they were. Some of 'em don't even know what they were accused of.'

'I'm glad you're free,' Jeb said.

'You're a good man, Mr Deeds.'

Ellie linked arms with her brother.

'Ain't many who would agree with that.' Jeb laughed.

'You sure you don't want us to hunt out this other one before we go?'

'Get a head start on that posse,' Jeb said. 'You can leave Tom Rider to me.'

Sunlight warmed the morning air as the men rode past. Tom crouched low and clung to the saloon wall to keep out of sight. Ellie's words echoed in his head. *Believes what people tell him; that don't do no one any good.*

'An hour's ride, half an hour's rest,' Ellie called after them.

On the other side of the square Brogan stood upright and leaned his head back against the post. He closed his eyes against the dust and let the sunlight fall on his face. Beside him, Bill Gifford looked in poor shape. His head lolled forward when he tried to keep it upright, his lips were cracked and his face was sallow. He tried to say something. Brogan opened his eyes and looked at him.

148

'Hey, Deeds,' Brogan shouted. 'This man needs water.'

Jeb looked at Ellie.

'Needs it but he don't deserve it,' she said.

Jeb disappeared into the saloon and came out with a ladle of water. He carried it carefully across the square and held it to Gifford's lips. He drank greedily but his eyes were dull and unfocused; his cheeks were gaunt. After he had finished drinking, his head lolled forward again.

Jeb put down the ladle, stepped round behind the post and cut Gifford loose. He toppled into a heap in the dirt. Jeb collected up the rope and nudged him with the toe of his boot.

'Get up and come inside with me now or I'll tie you up again.'

Jeb noticed Eli was missing: he must have crawled away somewhere. Gifford staggered to his feet. Jeb shoved him in the direction of the saloon. Doubled over, he stumbled forward. When his knees buckled, Jeb grabbed him to stop

149

him nosediving into the ground. He got as far as the porch, but the steps were too much for him.

Ellie stared down as Jeb tied Gifford by the leg to the rail close to the horse trough and the pile of coffins. Tight to the corner of the saloon wall, Tom was barely twenty feet away.

'What about me?' Brogan hollered. 'You gonna leave me here?'

Jeb crossed the square again.

'Now look, Jeb,' Brogan began as Jeb sawed through the rope which held him to the pillar. 'We can work this out, can't we?'

He hurried his words like a salesman anxious to close a deal.

'Known you a long time, Jeb,' Brogan whispered. 'Remember you as a kid. I was the one who persuaded Bill to let your pa have that piece of land so he could build a house for his family.'

Jeb ignored him.

'Otherwise, where would you kids have grown up?' Brogan rattled on. 'Ask Ellie, she'll agree with me. She did a fine job raising you boys. She had it tough, no mistake.'

The rope fell to the ground. Feeling the sudden freedom, Brogan lurched forward, raised a fist and spun round on Jeb.

'You little — '

Jeb was ready for him. His Colt was in his hand, aimed at Brogan's belly.

'Didn't mean nothing,' Brogan said quickly. His voice shook; he backed away.

'That was just — '

Jeb glared and gestured for him to walk towards the saloon. Brogan made a show of raising his hands above his head. While Jeb tied him to the rail alongside Bill Gifford, Ellie covered him with her Winchester.

'You got water right there,' Jeb said, indicating the trough. 'Seeing as you got to eat, I'll find you something.'

He fetched half a loaf from inside the saloon and tossed it down from the porch. The crust was brick-hard and the crumb was jade.

'Done any thinking yet, Brogan?'

'Come down here and talk to me, Jeb.' Brogan managed a smile. 'Man to man.'

'Too late,' Jeb said. 'You ain't been a man for a long time. A liar, maybe. A cheat. A thief. A murderer — '

'I built this town, boy,' Brogan roared. 'Me and Bill. If it wasn't for us and Tom Rider, there'd be nothing here but sand and tumbleweed.'

'Ain't interested in what you built, Brogan,' Jeb said. 'I know about that.'

'Well, what then?' Brogan whined.

'I told you. I'm waiting for your confession.'

Jeb's voice was as patient as if he had all the time in the world.

'Wait all you want,' Brogan spat. 'Brett and the posse will be back tonight. You may have taken their horses, but they're coming.'

Jeb's bootheels clicked on the wooden porch steps as he climbed down to face Brogan. His .45 was in his hand.

'I could shoot you right now,' Jeb

said. 'Get it done with.'

'Shoot me, Brett won't rest until you're dead. I made my son sheriff. Look what your pa made you.'

Jeb's hand tensed on the handle of his pistol.

'Jeb.' Ellie called him sharply. 'No sense in wasting your breath on him. If he ain't ready to confess, there ain't nothing to say.'

Tom shrank back against the side of the building. Was all this Ellie's idea? Was she the one who had planned for Jeb to empty the town while she got rid of the posse? If it was, she had done a good job. Even if Tom got to Bill Gifford, he was in no state to run. If he managed to free Brogan, how could they steal horses without being noticed?

Just as Tom was weighing the odds for and against getting help from the Gifford place, there was a noise behind him. He froze. He looked back over his shoulder, expecting to stare down the barrel of a .45. Behind him, crawling through the dirt on all fours was Eli.

Eli jerked his head, indicating for Tom to follow. They could hear Jeb's and Ellie's voices in the saloon.

Tom and Eli crawled backwards until they were behind the saloon. Eli got to his feet and tried the back door to the hardware store next door. Locked. He moved on to the next building, constantly glancing back over his shoulder. Tom followed. Every step they took they expected to turn and see Jeb right behind them.

A few buildings further on, someone had left a back door unlocked. The hinges screeched a warning as Eli inched open the door. There was a sudden thud and clatter above them; an ugly scratching noise made them look up. A black vulture sat on the edge of the roof and stared down at them. Its gnarled talons gripped the edge of the shingles; the breeze disturbed its ragged feathers.

Eli pulled at the door again. The hinges squealed. He looked at Tom. *Shall I go on with this?* Tom nodded.

One final pull and the door lurched open far enough for them to squeeze inside. The vulture's claws rattled on the shingles above them.

It was the storeroom for the old grocery; the owners had moved when bigger premises became available. Since then the building had stood empty. The place was dark and smelled of mice. The small window was layered in dirt and spiders' webs.

Another door led into the store itself. The old wooden counter was camouflaged in dust and the walls were lined with empty shelves. A chair stood in the corner dotted with woodworm holes. Filthy cotton blinds were pulled across the windows and blocked the view of the street. In here the light was decayed.

Tom crossed quickly to the window and held the blind away from the pane. Nothing. Just the coils of rope, the waiting coffins, Brogan and Gifford tied to the rail.

'What are we gonna do, Tom?' Fear

scratched Eli's voice.

Tom watched the vultures on the roof opposite. There were two of them now. Their little bald heads ducked and bobbed as they took in the scene below them. Their vicious beaks stabbed the air.

'Didn't even get to my horse before one of them jumped me,' Eli said. 'Thought they were going to string me up.'

'They ain't got nothing against you,' Tom said. 'They drove everyone away. Reckon Jeb expected you to run too.'

Tom let the blind fall back against the window. Dust puffed out into the air.

'You should go, Eli,' Tom said. 'If you slip out to the livery stable now, there won't be anyone to stop you.'

In the yellow light Eli's face was drawn and afraid.

'If Jeb had business with you, he would have tied you up like the others,' Tom continued.

'What about you, Tom?'

156

'Don't have a choice. This is something between me and the Deeds that goes back a long way. Still haven't figured it yet, but I'm beginning to.'

A mouse gnawed at a floorboard somewhere in the shadows. The tiny scuffling sound caught their attention for a second. They both turned their heads and listened.

'Don't feel right, Tom,' Eli said. 'A man should stand and fight alongside his friends.'

'Been sheriff for ten years,' Tom said. 'If it wasn't for my knees giving me gyp, I'd be sheriff for ten more. I've known Jeb and Ellie all that time. If there's anyone that can sort this out it's me.'

'They're mean as a basket of snakes,' Eli said. 'Everybody says so.'

'Known 'em since they were kids,' Tom said. 'You know what their pa was like. They didn't have a chance.'

There was a sound from outside, a cry which could have been the wind. Above the noise of their conversation and their footsteps on the boards of the empty room, they hardly heard it. Tom moved the blind again and peered into the square. The moan came again.

It was a human voice. A weak cry. Someone was calling Tom's name.

'Don't go out there,' Eli said.

Tom listened hard.

'It's a trap,' Eli said. 'Got to be.'

'Was it Bill?' Tom said.

They stood still and tried not to hear their own breathing or the thud of their heartbeats.

'I'll go,' Eli said. 'If they ain't interested in me, I'll be fine. I'll slip out the back again.'

Eli's boots echoed as he strode across the wooden floor. Tom watched him. He pulled open the door to the storeroom and then pushed the outside door. The hinges screamed.

'Hello, Eli.'

It was Jeb's voice, calm and confident, as if he had arranged to meet Eli there. Eli stopped, framed in the doorway against the bright daylight. He turned to where Jeb stood.

'Tom Rider in there?'

Eli hesitated. In that second, Jeb knew.

'Got no quarrel with you, Eli,' Jeb said. 'Why didn't you take off along with all the others? I gave you the chance.'

'No reason to take off, Jeb,' Eli said. 'Ain't doing no harm here.'

As he spoke, Eli's hand inched towards the handle of his Colt.

Jeb must have seen it. 'Ain't going to draw on me are you, Eli?'

He asked the question calmly; there was a note of surprise in his voice.

As Tom saw Eli's hand tighten on the handle of his gun, a pistol shot split the air. Eli didn't have time to draw. He doubled over and toppled into the sunlight.

Tom's gun was in his hand now.

'You in there, Tom?' Jeb shouted.

He knew better than to step into the doorway and frame himself against the light. Tom froze.

'He was trying to draw on me, Tom. You saw that.'

Tom backed towards the shop door

which opened onto the square. He kept his eyes on the slab of sunlight which fell over Eli's body; he watched for the slightest movement, the faintest flicker of a shadow which would tell him Jeb was coming.

Tom felt for the handle and pulled. The hinges were stiff with lack of use. He kept his eyes on the back doorway. If he could slip round the side of the building, he might be able to get the drop on Jeb.

'Tom,' Jeb called again. 'You got to be in there.'

The front door gave. Tom felt a draught of fresh air on his neck. He pulled the door open and stepped backwards onto the porch. At the same time, he felt a gun barrel jab him between the shoulder blades.

'Drop your gun, Tom. Then turn round real slow.'

Tom let his .45 clatter onto the porch. He raised his hands and turned. Ellie was there with her Winchester pointed at his chest.

10

No one had swept up the broken glass and the upturned tables were shoved aside. Three chairs stood with their backs to the bar. Tom sat in one of the chairs while Ellie kept him covered. Her intelligent eyes read his face. Neither of them wasted energy talking. Tom was grateful for a chair after hours of crouching by the saloon wall; the old pain burned in his knee joints.

Jeb hauled Bill Gifford into the room by his collar. He shoved him into the chair next to Tom and went to fetch Brogan. Gifford's face was grey and his lips were dry; the night spent tied to a post had taken its toll.

Brogan staggered in with Jeb's .45 jammed in his kidneys. His face burned with unconcealed rage; he was just managing to hold his tongue.

Halfway across the empty bar room

Jeb set up two chairs, which faced the three men. Ellie kept her Winchester trained on them while he went outside again. This time he came in with a pile of sheriff's record books.

'I don't know what you think you're doing — ' Brogan began.

He stuck a thumb in his vest pocket next to his watch chain, his old gesture of self-importance.

Ellie ratcheted back the hammer of the Winchester and turned the barrel on him. Brogan's voice died.

Jeb began sorting the pile of record books into the order he wanted. He worked his way through them, opened them at the pages he required and laid them face down, one on top of the other.

'Bill Gifford needs a drink of water,' Tom said.

'Just like you, Tom. Making sure folks are looked after,' Ellie said. 'Making sure the whole town is nice as apple pie.'

Her words were steel. Tom was taken

aback. Why should she say this?

'I'll fetch it,' Jeb snapped.

Ellie sat down and rested the Winchester in her lap. Once Gifford had a glass of water in his hand, Jeb sat beside her.

'Time for the reckoning,' Jeb said. 'Time for us to get to the truth of things.'

Brogan exploded. 'This is a trick,' he snarled. 'You scare the townspeople away, you steal the posse's horses. What do you mean, 'a reckoning'?'

'You ain't got no right to do this.' Gifford joined in. His voice was weak and clawed at his throat, but the water and Brogan's confidence revived him.

Jeb ignored them and turned to the pile of sheriff's records beside his chair.

'This is a good one.' He started to read. ''Storekeeper complained Jeb Deeds stole two candy canes. Found Jeb and Ellie Deeds in livery. Sent them home.' Remember that, Tom?'

Tom nodded.

'Here's another one.' Jeb flicked

through the pages. 'Jeb Deeds riding Mrs Perkins's sow down Main Street. Returned pig. Made him apologize.'

Ellie laughed.

'Know why Jeb stole that candy?' Ellie said. 'It was my birthday. He told me to wait in the hayloft because he had a surprise for me.'

'Know why I took that sow?' Jeb said. 'I asked Ma Perkins for a slice of bread. She told me I was a greedy little pig, so I thought I'd teach her a lesson.'

Brogan looked sour now.

'What is this? You telling us what hard times you had when you were kids? Every kid's got stories like that.'

'Came across 'em in Tom's books,' Jeb said. 'They made me smile.'

'That may look charming now,' Brogan continued. 'You Deeds kids ran wild. You may think helping yourself to a candy cane is amusing. What it means is you didn't know right from wrong.'

'Had no one to teach 'em,' Gifford said. His voice rasped in his throat. 'I showed kindness to their father. Gave him a place to raise his kids. Gave him a job. Turned out he was a worthless drunk and worse.'

Colour drained from Jeb's face. His fingers tightened on the book in his hand. Ellie touched him lightly on the arm.

'Anything else?' Ellie said.

'How long have you got?' Gifford crowed. 'Lazy, incompetent, useless, let his kids run wild — '

Gifford's list ended in an explosive coughing fit. Ellie kept hold of Jeb's arm.

'You started off as partners. Ain't that right?'

'We were never partners,' Gifford said coldly. 'Your pa worked for me.'

'In the early days, before the town was built,' Ellie said. 'Before Tom Rider was sheriff.'

'Not even then,' Gifford said.

'What is this?' Brogan snarled. 'Who are you to be asking questions? Me and Bill created this town. Planned it and built it. Then I became mayor and Bill

165

ran his cattle business. Your pa used to string along with us while we let him.'

'That ain't right,' Jeb said. 'He used to tell us you all picked this spot because it was on the Butterfield route from Fort Highsmith to Los Enganos.'

'So what?' Brogan said.

'So you could rob the stage,' Jeb said calmly. 'You made out you were honest settlers building houses and raising a herd. There were so many lawbreakers down here in those days, nobody noticed you. Riders used to sweep in from West Texas and raise Cain; bank robbers from Juarez hid out in the caves south of Baldy Peak. Everyone knows the stories.'

'You hear these stories, Tom?' Ellie waved the Winchester in his direction.

'I heard 'em,' Tom said. 'But this was before I arrived.'

'And it never occurred to you to ask who put up the money to start building the town?'

'It was a cattle town,' Tom said. 'Before the railhead was built, cowboys rested up here after the drives.' He gave a shrug. 'The ranches were successful,' he went on. 'Bill owned the biggest of 'em. Traders came and the town grew.'

'Never occurred to you that the traders had stores already built, which they could lease from Mayor Brogan?' Ellie said. 'Never occurred to you that no other cow town had a saloon with a crystal chandelier and a French piano?'

Tom hesitated. It hadn't occurred to him. When he arrived, El Cobarde was booming. Carpenters were at work. Cattle drives were passing through. The place was a hive of activity. When he was appointed sheriff there was so much to do he didn't have time to enquire into who built which property before he arrived. When the railway came, the place exploded. This was one of the most prosperous towns south of the Trans Pecos. Tom threw his life into running it well.

'Now you're asking Tom about what happened before he even lived here?' Brogan snapped. 'What is this?'

'The robberies were just small-time, weren't they, Brogan?' Jeb said. 'Purses, watches, a few handfuls of bills.' He watched Brogan's face. 'All except the last one.'

'You're dreaming,' Brogan said. 'Where did you get all this about robbing stages, anyhow?'

'Reason you're a successful man is you always quit while you're ahead,' Ellie said. 'Your downfall is you're a cheat and a murdering liar and the truth has a way of finding people like you out.'

'If you weren't pointing a Winchester at me, you couldn't get away with this. You're scum, just like your pa.'

Jeb let Brogan sound off. The insults glanced off him. He didn't even look at the mayor. Instead, he dug his hand deep into his pants pocket and fished out a gold coin. He held it out on his palm with the twin-headed eagle showing.

'Recognize this?'

'Carson City gold,' Brogan said.

'Where did you get hold of that?'

'Same place you got yours,' Jeb said. He flipped the coin over to Tom. 'Read out the date.'

Tom peered at the coin.

He looked up at Jeb. '1869. So what?'

'Now look at Brogan's.'

'You're crazy,' Brogan exploded. 'You think I carry gold coins around with me?'

'It's on his watch chain,' Jeb said calmly.

'Let me look,' Tom said.

'You planning to steal watches now?' Brogan sneered.

He freed the chain from the buttonhole of his vest and handed it to Tom. A gold coin hung from the chain.

'Same date,' Tom confirmed.

Jeb turned to Gifford.

'Now let him see yours.'

'Don't have to,' Gifford said. 'It's the same.'

Ellie waved the barrel of the Winchester at him. Gifford unhooked his watch chain and handed it to Tom. Tom inspected the coin on the chain before handing it back.

'Coincidence?' Jeb asked him. 'What do you think, Tom?'

'Of course it's a coincidence,' Brogan blustered. 'You ain't explained what you're doing with a gold coin, anyway.'

'My pa gave it to me the night he died,' Jeb said. 'Said it was all the proof I'd ever need. He told me one day you'd try to cheat him. Said you'd cheat me too if I gave you the chance.'

'What nonsense is this?' Brogan said.

Jeb ignored him. 'Take another look at the coin, Tom. See anything scratched there?'

Tom held the coin up to catch the light from the window. If he squinted he could just make out some clumsy letters scored with the tip of a blade.

'Looks like a D, an H. Then there's something I can't read.'

'Compare it with the others, Tom,' Jeb said.

Brogan slapped his watch chain into Tom's hand.

'This is foolery, Tom. I'm telling you.'

Tom screwed up his eyes and held the coin up to the light. Then he did the same for Bill Gifford's.

'D, H, W,' he said. 'On all three.'

'What does this prove?' Brogan ran a finger round the collar of his shirt as if it was suddenly too tight. 'This is a pantomime.'

'Shut up, Brogan,' Gifford said.

He looked at Tom, then at Jeb.

'This was all a long time ago, more than ten years. Your pa told you, did he?'

There was weariness in Bill Gifford's face.

'We were poor then. We had no money to get started. Me, Brogan and your pa all arrived down here together. You Deeds, Brett and my Johnny were all kids. We knew we could make a fortune here. Miles of open range just right for longhorns, clear route north to Kansas, plenty of space and fresh spring water. Just the right place to build a town.'

Gifford paused.

'You don't understand. We did what we had to. So we held up a few Butterfields. So what? Nobody got hurt. Look what came of it. Look around you at this town. Look at my ranch. We built an empire out of nothing. We created homes and jobs — '

'And you got rich,' Ellie said.

'We worked hard. We always did. There ain't been a day — '

'You're a fool, Bill,' Brogan interrupted. 'Just button it.'

'What are the letters?' Tom said.

'Can't you guess?' Gifford said. 'We were cock-a-hoop. We'd held up a bullion stage and got away with it. Do you know how much gold was in those strongboxes?'

'D, H, W,' Ellie said. 'Donnal Brogan, Hank Deeds, William Gifford. That's right, ain't it?'

'No one was going to suspect us,' Gifford went on. 'We were careful. We didn't spend the money. We hid it and waited. Other gangs used to ride through, shooting up the place, drawing attention to themselves. But not us. We didn't do nothing. Just carried on with our daily lives. Even my Annie didn't know anything about it.'

Jeb turned his attention to Tom. 'What do you think about that? The men who robbed the bullion stage are the ones who hired you as sheriff.'

Tom was silent. He stared first at Gifford, then Brogan.

'Don't look at me like that, Tom. Don't you come high and mighty with me. I've paid you good wages for a long time. If it wasn't for me and Bill taking a risk when we were young, you'd still be working for the railway company now.'

'You ain't denying it?' Tom said. 'I heard about that robbery. The whole of Texas did. The bank hired out posses and bounty hunters from all over. Trailed the Fletcher gang to some caves in the mountains. Hung all five of 'em for it, didn't they?'

Brogan looked sideways at Bill Gifford.

'I don't remember.'

Gifford shifted in his chair and stared at the floor. Ellie lay the Winchester across her knees.

'Don't worry,' she said gently. 'We ain't concerned with them.'

'Pa told me you'd cheat us,' Jeb said. 'He was right, wasn't he?'

'What do you mean?' Brogan said. 'Are you after blackmail money? You threatening to go to the sheriff with a few scratched coins and a story about a robbery which everyone's forgot about?' Brogan threw his head back and laughed. 'You remember who the sheriff is? Even if you go all the way to the state governor's office, nobody's going to believe a lowlife son of a cattle hand. Nobody's going to care.'

'We ain't going nowhere,' Jeb said.

'Then what's all this about?'

Ellie pointed the Winchester at Brogan.

'What did happen to all that gold, Mayor Brogan?'

'Buried it. Left it underground for

years. None of us touched it.'

'Is it still there?' Ellie said innocently.

'I knew it,' Brogan snarled. 'It's the money you want. You're just like us.'

Ellie snapped back the hammer of the Winchester and raised it level with Brogan's chest.

'We're nothing like you. Never were. Never will be.'

'I only meant — ' Brogan said.

'It ain't still there,' Gifford interrupted.

His eyes were hollow; his words dried his throat. He looked ill. 'We dug it up — '

'Changed the gold for dollars,' Brogan broke in. 'Paid the carpenters who built this town. Paid for the saloon you're sitting in right now. Paid the wages men raised families on. How many more times?'

'And where was this gold buried, exactly?' Jeb said.

Gifford looked aside.

'It was a long time ago,' Brogan said. 'I don't remember.'

'I remember,' Jeb said. 'By the river, where there's a line of screw beans and walnut trees along the bank.'

'How would you know that?' Brogan sneered. 'You were a kid.'

'I was there the night you dug it up. I saw both of you.'

'Why would you remember a thing like that?'

Jeb stared at them both and didn't answer.

11

Early afternoon heat entered the saloon. The wooden walls were warm to the touch; the air smelled of dust. Particles danced in the sunlight in front of the window. The carpet of smashed glass sparked like jewellery and rasped against the floorboards every time anyone moved their feet.

Outside, a committee of vultures gathered along the ridge of the roofs on the opposite side of the square. They waited, watched and patiently anticipated disaster. Their heavy black overcoats shone under the beating sun; the birds gave no sign of wanting to seek out shade.

Sensing a disturbance in the air, the vultures turned their heads sharply. A faint dust cloud rose somewhere near the horizon; someone was coming. The cloud was too far away to concern them yet: the birds turned back to the square and watched in case anyone left the saloon.

'You saw everything?'

Tom pushed his chair back; glass crunched underneath his boots.

'Why didn't you . . . ?'

'Come forward?' Jeb said. He stared at Tom. 'After what I saw, all the blood was scared out of me. I was nine years old. You were the sheriff who threatened to lock me in jail when I stole a sugar candy from the grocery. How could I tell you?'

'Besides that, I told him not to,' Ellie said.

She rested the Winchester on her knees again. The barrel pointed at Tom.

'You don't know how afeared we were. We liked you when we were kids, Tom. We respected you. We were a little scared of you, maybe, but this was different.'

She paused. 'This was a nightmare. I knew that if we talked we could get ourselves killed just like pa. So I took

Jeb and we snuck away in the night and buried our secret, just like pa buried his gold. We ain't never dug it up till now.'

'What is she talking about?' Brogan appealed to the others. 'Burying a secret? Snuck away in the night? Is this some kind of fairy tale?'

'Wait a minute.' Tom caught on. 'You're saying you were there too? You saw what Jeb saw?'

'This is funny,' Brogan said. 'We're talking about what a couple of kids say they saw in the pitch dark one night ten years ago.'

'Why didn't you say nothing till now?' Tom said.

'We had to survive,' Ellie said fiercely. Her hand rested on the Winchester. 'I had the boys to look after. They were wild even when times was good. After Ma died I had to do everything. Just keeping 'em fed was hard enough.'

'You received regular handouts from the ranch,' Gifford broke in. 'We never let anyone starve.'

Ellie ignored him.

'The boys were always in trouble. Who was going to believe us?'

'And what did you do?' Brogan sneered. 'Got your claws into Brett as soon as you could. You knew a good thing when you saw it.'

Ellie stared at him coldly.

'I knew everyone would say that about me. Truth is, I was lonely and young and he was a handsome boy. I didn't know what a lazy, selfish pig you'd brought him up to be.'

Blood pumped into Brogan's face. 'You little . . . How dare you say that?'

'It's the truth. My pa was weak and foolish so I know what a weak and foolish man looks like,' Ellie said. 'The difference is, my pa loved his family; Brett only loves himself.'

Ellie steadied the Winchester. Brogan clenched his fists until the knuckles whitened.

'This is bull,' Brogan said. 'You're a Deeds through and through. A liar and a coward, just like your pa. If you weren't behind that rifle you wouldn't have the nerve.'

Ellie stood the rifle on the floor beside her and stared at Brogan. 'What I'm saying is the truth.'

Outside the window across the square the vultures were watching. Brogan stood up.

'I've had enough.'

'Sit down,' Tom said. 'Let her have her say.'

'Tom's right,' Gifford said. 'Hear her out.'

Ellie picked up her rifle again and rested it across her knees.

'Tell us,' Tom said. 'What did you see that night?'

'She saw exactly what I saw,' Jeb said. 'If we tell you, Tom, chances are you won't believe us.'

'I'll be the judge of that,' Tom said.

'It was getting dark,' Jeb began. 'We were at home. Pa said he had to go out somewhere. He pulled this gold coin out of his pocket and gave it to me. He'd shown it to us before; he'd told us the story of the gold he'd buried with Brogan and Gifford a hundred times. 'We're gonna be rich some day,' he used to say.'

Tom leaned forward intent on every word. Brogan stretched his legs in front of him and fiddled with his watch chain. Gifford stared out of the window.

'He thought something was going to happen,' Jeb continued. 'That's why he gave me the coin. He told me to stay in the house with Ellie. Said he'd be back late — '

'Telling him what to do never worked with Jeb,' Ellie broke in. 'Tell him to do one thing and you could be sure he'd do the opposite.'

Jeb grinned at her. 'Anyhow, I sneaked out after Pa.'

'As soon as I realized he was missing, I followed,' Ellie said.

'Pa picked up a spade and headed out to the river,' Jeb continued. 'Ended up where there's an avenue of walnuts. It's a beautiful spot. He used to take me fishing there. Someone had started to build a house: there were piles of timber everywhere. The porch was half-built and a whole bunch of roof shingles was missing. 'Course, I didn't know whose house it was.'

Jeb cleared his throat. Maybe it was the dust in the air, maybe it was thinking about all this. Tom couldn't tell.

'I hung back and hid in the brush. I was scared Pa would see me. He looked around for a while, then he started digging . . . ' Jeb hesitated. 'A woman came out from behind the trees. She must have been down by the river all along. I didn't know who she was.'

Tom sat back in his chair. 'You saw Elizabeth?'

'I didn't know who it was back then,' Jeb said.

'Where is all this getting us?' Brogan interrupted angrily. 'So he hid in the bushes when he was a kid. So what? No one can remember what they saw ten years ago.'

'Shut up, Brogan,' Gifford said. 'He

183

can remember just fine.'

Ellie's hand moved on the Winchester in case Brogan should think of standing up again.

'The woman talked to Pa. I wasn't close enough to hear.'

'I found Jeb crouching down behind a box thorn,' Ellie interrupted. 'I guess the woman was asking Pa what he was doing. He had a spade in his hand; there was a pile of earth beside him. I remember she was laughing.'

'Laughing?' Tom said.

'She showed him some plants she'd put in the ground over by the new house. There was dirt on her hands.'

'Magnolias,' Tom said. 'She'd planted them on either side of the porch steps that afternoon.'

'Elizabeth had a good sense of humour,' Bill said. 'I remember that.'

'Probably making a joke of your pa digging her garden for her,' Tom said. 'It's the kind of thing she would have done.'

The vultures stood guard along the

rooftop on the opposite side of the square. There were more of them now, lined up with their shoulders hunched and their untidy feathers gleaming in the sunlight. Their bald heads swivelled and jerked as they kept watch; their beaks were ready.

'We watched Pa talking to the lady for a while. It was fun to be spying on them with them not knowing we were there. Then the lady went into the half-built house. Pa carried on digging. We were just about to leave when the riders came,' Ellie said.

'Two of them from the direction of town,' Jeb said. 'They had masks pulled up over their faces.'

'It was getting dark by this time,' Ellie broke in. 'The sun was setting right behind the house. It was like the sky was on fire. You could hear the swish of rushes down on the riverbank and the cicadas in the trees.'

'The riders slipped down off their horses. They were mad as hell. 'Why didn't you wait for us?' one of 'em was shouting. Pa was telling 'em he hadn't meant no harm. He just arrived early and started to dig. One of 'em was shouting that you could never trust a Deeds. What did he think he was playing at?' Jeb fell silent for a moment. 'Right then I knew I couldn't do nothing about it, but I would one day. They treated my pa like dirt.'

Jeb stared at Brogan and then at Gifford. Brogan met his gaze; Gifford looked away.

'Pa started to argue with 'em like he was trying to tell 'em something, but they wouldn't listen. With all the noise, the woman came out onto the porch then. She was holding a rifle. Pa shouted something to her. She screamed when she saw the men in the masks. Pa was shouting and the woman was scream- ing. She fired the rifle up in the air. Guess she wanted to scare 'em.'

Jeb stopped again. The black vultures jostled for position on the building across from the saloon.

'Go on,' Tom said softly. 'Finish it.'

'One of them drew,' Ellie said.

More vultures joined the line.

'Aimed at the woman and fired.'

Tom gasped as though he had just taken a punch in the gut.

'She fell right there on the porch. I didn't know what to do then. I just clung on to Jeb and kept real quiet. I was making sure Jeb was ducked down out of sight, then there was another shot.'

Ellie picked up the Winchester, cocked it and pointed it at Brogan.

'One of 'em shot Pa.'

'Now wait a minute,' Brogan said. 'These guys were wearing masks, you said so yourself. It was dark. It was a long time ago. You can't accuse me now.'

Ellie ignored him. 'They both had firearms in their hands,' she said. 'But I'm guessing it was this one.'

'Guessing?' Brogan spat. 'Guessing?'

'Leave it,' Gifford said.

'They ain't got proof.' Brogan laughed. 'They ain't got nothing.'

'They pulled the Butterfield chest out of the ground and filled in the hole,' Ellie said. 'They made it look like an animal had been digging there. They used Pa's shovel. I can tell you my heart was pounding so hard, I thought I was going to pass out.'

'Baloney,' Brogan said. 'You ain't buying this, are you, Tom? Masked men on a dark night. Nothing but foolishness.'

'Hard work shovelling dirt when you're in a hurry, ain't it, Brogan?' Ellie went on. 'You need to breathe deep.' She stared at Tom.

'They took their masks off,' Ellie said simply. 'That's how I know it was them.'

'I saw them,' Jeb said. 'Ellie made me look. Told me I was never to forget who I saw that night.'

Tom stared ahead of him. Gifford's eyes were on the floor. Brogan leaned back in his chair and tucked a thumb into his vest pocket.

'You're forgetting something,' Brogan

said. 'At the time, the sheriff concluded that Hank Deeds had gone round to ask Elizabeth for food for his children, which he sometimes did. Because it was dark he frightened her and she shot him. He fired back. It was a tragic accident. You'll be able to read about it in one of those sheriff's record books he was so fond of keeping.'

'I've read it,' Jeb said. 'It also says no gun was found on Hank Deeds's body.'

'It never made any sense,' Tom said.

Everyone turned to look at him.

'That's what it says at the end of the entry. 'The explanation don't make any sense.''

'Pa never carried a gun,' Ellie said. 'He kept it hung up on a beam in the house where none of us kids could reach it.'

Brogan kicked a few pieces of broken glass away from under his chair. The scuttling sound made everyone look down at the floor.

'Still ain't no proof,' Brogan said. 'It's just guesswork.'

'Don't you talk to me, Brogan,' Tom said. 'Don't you come near me. Don't you even look at me.'

Brogan laughed.

'You're a fool, Tom. You were a fool then and you're a fool now. Writing everything down in your record books. 'The explanation don't make any sense'? What kind of lawman writes that?'

'The honest kind,' Gifford said. 'We never intended any of this, Tom. It was a mistake. If that fool Hank Deeds had waited for us like we told him to, none of it would have happened. We would have seen Elizabeth was there. We would have left the box buried, gone home and come back when she wasn't around.'

He appealed to Tom. 'You know we never would have intended anything like that. But she'd seen the Butterfield chest. We couldn't have anyone knowing about the holdup. We didn't know you were going to pick a piece of land to build on right where we'd buried the gold.'

'So you shot her.'

'That was our one chance, right there in our hands,' Gifford went on. 'It was the future. Ours, yours, everybody's. We knew we'd never get another. Easiest thing to do was make it look as though Elizabeth and Deeds had shot each other and pin the blame on Deeds.'

Gifford's eyes slid away from Tom.

'Like I said,' he murmured, 'it was never intended.'

Brogan kicked away a piece of broken glass and glared at Tom.

'Don't you stand in judgment,' he sneered. 'You earned a fat living from us all these years. Room and board at the saloon all paid for. Salary twice what any other sheriff makes. You didn't turn none of that down.'

'I didn't know,' Tom said. 'How could I?'

'Hear that, Jeb?' Brogan said. 'The sheriff didn't know: the brave sheriff who broke up bar fights and faced down rustlers; honest Tom, who wrote everything in his record book so he

191

could always be held to account.'

Brogan looked at Jeb.

'Why didn't he know who killed your pa? Why didn't he know who killed his own wife?'

Brogan thrust out his jaw. A smile twisted the corner of his bruised mouth.

'Because he didn't ask.' Brogan paused like a poker player showing a winning hand.

'He was busy feeling sorry for himself,' he went on. 'Chasing small-time crooks and being Honest Tom whom everybody in El Cobarde looked up to and respected. He was so busy holding his hand out for his paycheck that he didn't bother to look at what was right under his nose.'

With a wild yell Tom launched himself on Brogan. The chair toppled backwards as Tom drew back his fist and slugged Brogan a hammer punch in the jaw. There was a vicious snapping sound and Brogan spat teeth. The men wrestled, kicked and punched at each other. As Tom hooked back his arm for another blow, Gifford grabbed it and flung him backwards across the floor.

A rifle shot made them freeze. Ellie and Jeb were on their feet and had them covered. A trickle of plaster dust fell from a neat bullet hole in the ceiling.

'Enough,' Ellie yelled. 'I ain't allowing you the satisfaction, Tom.'

As Brogan struggled to his feet Ellie swung the butt of the Winchester into the side of his head. His legs jellified under him and he crashed face down onto the floor.

'Ellie,' Gifford shouted. He stared at her open-mouthed.

Before he had time to think she raised the rifle butt and slammed it into his temple. He toppled over Brogan like a felled tree.

Tom backed away, his hands outstretched towards her. Ellie swung the gun round and pointed the barrel at him. She pulled back the hammer.

'You ain't so different, Tom,' Ellie

said. 'You ain't the same but you ain't so different. They're gutless murdering scum on the outside, you're gutless on the inside where no one can see. Me and Jeb are doing what a decent sheriff should have done years ago.'

She yelled to Jeb to fetch rope from outside. When he brought it, he threw it on the floor and kicked it over to Tom.

'Tie their hands behind their backs real tight,' Ellie snapped, 'while I make up my mind what to do with you.'

12

The line of vultures bobbed their heads with interest as Jeb hauled Brogan and then Gifford outside. They lay like bulging sacks on the porch, their eyelids flickering, blood on their faces. Ellie stood in the doorway and covered Tom with her Winchester.

Jeb stared at the trussed bodies; neither approval nor disapproval registered on his face. Maybe he was thinking of his pa. Ellie glanced at him; they had talked about this moment for so long.

Jeb stepped down off the porch and crossed the square to where a cart stood with its shafts resting on the ground. The big wheels were greased and moved easily. He hauled it across the square and set it to rest in front of the saloon. The noise disturbed Brogan, who groaned on the edge of consciousness.

Jeb picked up two of the lengths of rope which lay in the dirt beside the coffins. He checked the nooses, looped the ropes over his arm and climbed back onto the porch.

'Best get this on 'em before they wake up.'

Ellie said nothing. She kept the Winchester pointed at Tom.

Jeb lifted Gifford's head, shoved a noose over it and wrestled it tight. Gifford's eyes were closed, his breathing was hoarse in his throat. Then Jeb let the head drop with a thud onto the boards of the porch. When he tried the same with Gifford the mayor's eyes flicked open, the pupils rolled back under his skull. A noise like the creak of a hinge came from his throat.

'You ain't going through with this, Jeb?' Tom said. 'You got more decency than that.'

Jeb ignored him. He heaved Gifford over his shoulder, carried him down the porch steps, backed up to the tail of the wagon and dropped him. His skull

196

cracked against the wood.

Brogan was heavier; added to this he was starting to move. He pulled at the rope around his wrists and squirmed onto his side as if he could roll himself out of the noose. Jeb stared down at him with contempt.

Tom stiffened in his seat.

'Jeb, you can't . . . ' Tom began.

Jeb slipped his hands under Brogan's shoulders and heaved him down the steps to the cart. Ellie kept the Winchester trained on Tom. Jeb collected the loose ends of the rope and slung them over the side of the cart.

'You can't do this, Jeb,' Tom said.

Ellie waved the rifle barrel, sat him in a chair and kept the Winchester trained on him while Jeb tied his hands behind his back.

In the cart, Brogan started to groan again. Gifford was out cold.

The upper room where Brogan had hidden was fronted by a balcony where customers had sat in the shade and enjoyed a view of the bustling square.

Three heavy pine pillars supported the roof above. Jeb took the two ropes and lobbed them round the central pillar, so that they fell into the street. He picked them up and tied them tight to the fat iron hooks which were screwed to the oak sides of the cart. Previously, the hooks had supported twenty-gallon water barrels; nothing would shift them. Brogan groaned again.

'I'll head over to the livery and fetch the horses,' Jeb said.

'Jeb,' Tom called. 'Please.'

Jeb turned away.

When he was across the square, Tom appealed to Ellie.

'You ain't going to let him do this?'

'Why shouldn't I? If you'd done your job properly, this is exactly what the judge would have done. You know it.'

'Then wait for a judge,' Tom said. 'Hold a trial.'

'And ask the sheriff to arrest them first?' Ellie laughed. 'These two had this town sewn up from the beginning. As long as nobody asked any questions, the sun shone every day. You wrote up all the misdemeanours in your record books; Bill Gifford sold his longhorns; Brogan congratulated himself on how prosperous he was.'

'Ellie, please . . . ' Tom tried to interrupt.

'That is, unless you were a Deeds. My pa was desperate. Being desperate made him team up with these two snakes. He was weak and foolish but they murdered him when he stood in their way, just like they murdered your Elizabeth.'

Tom was silent. His life had crumbled. The respect the townsfolk had for him, the esteem in which the mayor held him, his reputation for fairness and bravery, the courage he showed when Elizabeth died: all of it was hollow, founded on lies and meant nothing. Jeb and Ellie said he was a coward; Brogan called him a fool. Had he really looked away? Had he really allowed Brogan and Bill Gifford to mislead him all these years? *The explanation don't make any sense.*

He'd written the words himself. He'd known something was wrong; he never asked what it was.

This was the reckoning Jeb talked about. This was where Tom looked himself in the face. He had allowed Brogan to mislead him; he had allowed Gifford to flatter him. He blamed Hank Deeds, just like they wanted him to. All the time he had known he should ask questions because the explanation didn't make any sense. It took two scared kids hiding in the dark to make him see.

'This is justice,' Ellie said. 'You hand this over to our fine new sheriff, how far are you going to get?'

There was no answer; Tom felt as broken as if he was lying in the cart alongside Brogan and Gifford.

Memories of evenings right here on this porch filled Tom's head, Brogan and Gifford with their fists round tumblers of bourbon, Tom with his glass of iced lemon water in his hand. They exchanged news about the day:

Bill would tell them about his beeves; Brogan would update them on some new building project; Tom would describe disputes he had settled or infringements of the bylaws he had solved.

Tom remembered how Brogan was quick to organize wagonloads of timber to be delivered as soon as Elizabeth picked out the spot by the river for their house, and how Bill Gifford had volunteered his men to help Tom build the place. Elizabeth's design was ambitious; the project had taken longer than they anticipated. That meant there was always someone at the site; the men worked late into the evenings.

Elizabeth had died on a Sunday night, the one day of the week the site had been deserted. She had left Tom writing up his record books and ridden out after church with some young magnolias so that she could plant them without getting in the way of the men working the following day. Tom had said he would join her later.

'What was she wearing?' Tom asked.

Ellie was leaning back against the porch post with the Winchester still trained on him.

'That night,' Tom continued. 'What was Elizabeth wearing?'

Ellie was quiet for a minute. She stared at him.

'Is this a test?' Ellie said. 'To see if I was there?'

'What was she wearing that night?' Tom repeated.

'An orange shawl,' Ellie said. 'The colour of flame.'

'It was what she always wore to church,' Tom said. 'Every Sunday.'

A great weight pressed down across his shoulders as if he was supporting one of the beams of the house to stop the whole building toppling down on him. It took all his strength to hold it there.

'You believe us now?' Ellie said.

Tom's throat was dry.

'Reckon I always did.'

Jeb led two ponies across the square from the livery stable. He had the wagon harness and reins slung over his shoulder. Without looking up at Tom or Ellie, he tied the ponies to the porch rail and hung the reins and harness over the side of the wagon.

Brogan moaned. His moan turned into a gasp as air scratched at his lungs. He came to for a minute.

'Water.'

The word hung on his parched lips.

'Water.'

Jeb ignored him and climbed the porch steps.

Ellie turned to Tom. 'Want to take some to him?'

The row of vultures shuffled along the roofline. They arranged and re-arranged their feathers, ducked their heads and never took their eyes off the bodies in the wagon or the ropes which trailed over the high porch-post.

Brogan drifted into unconsciousness again. The square was silent.

'What are you planning, Jeb?' Tom

said. 'I mean, what do you want out of all this?'

'What Pa would have wanted,' Jeb said.

'And what's that?'

'Quit asking, Tom. That ain't your place right now.'

Jeb turned into the saloon. His boot-heels splintered the broken glass.

'What about you, Ellie?' Tom said.

'I want what's ours,' Ellie reflected. 'What Pa would have left to us.'

Jeb strolled out onto the porch with a bottle of red-eye in his hand. He yanked out the cork with his teeth, spat it onto the porch and took a pull at the whiskey.

Ellie flared. 'I ain't having that.'

She made a grab for the bottle and knocked it out of Jeb's hand. It rolled across the porch, spraying whiskey into the dust.

'Hey!' Jeb protested.

'You need something to steady your nerves, you take a good deep breath of fresh air,' Ellie said.

The hooch trickled out of the bottle and made a lake in the dust.

Ellie waved the Winchester dangerously. 'I mean it. That was what Pa did. I ain't having you going the same way.'

'Ellie,' Jeb pleaded.

This was how it had always been: Ellie in charge, doing the thinking and the planning and doing her best to stop Jeb getting into trouble.

One of the men down in the wagon groaned. Brogan was trying to lever himself into a sitting position. With his hands tied behind him and the heavy noose round his throat, he could hardly move. Eventually he was able to half-sit, half-lean against the side of the wagon. His eyes went wild as he registered where he was. Then he focused on Tom.

'Tom, for pity's sake.'

The words scratched in his mouth.

'He can't help you, Brogan.'

'Ellie,' Brogan said. 'Is that you?'

'Quit play-acting, Brogan,' Ellie snapped. 'You know who it is.'

Jeb leaned over the porch rail and

stared down into the wagon.

'Getting ready to hang, Brogan?'

Brogan stared helplessly up at him.

'After we hang you, we're gonna burn the town. When the posse gets back all they're going to find is you and Gifford swinging from the saloon porch and the black ruins of where they used to live. We'll be long gone.'

'We never said nothing about burning the town,' Ellie snapped. 'We want what's owed, that's all.'

Jeb rounded on her.

'Brogan and Gifford will pass on their fortunes to their sons. Johnny Gifford will have the biggest ranch within a three-day ride; Brett is sheriff. We ain't got no chance.'

'I can make you an offer,' Brogan said.

His voice was so hoarse that at first they hardly heard him.

'What can you offer us?' Ellie said.

'Untie me,' Brogan said. 'Then I'll tell you.' His voice was close to a whisper.

'Quite an operator, ain't he?' Jeb sneered. 'Rope round his neck and he's still trying to cut a deal.'

'At least give me a drink of water,' Brogan said.

'What are you offering, Brogan?' Ellie said.

'I can tell you where your pa's share of the gold is.'

They stared at him. Jeb stood up straight. The Winchester wavered in Ellie's hands. Brogan lay awkwardly in the cart, propped up on an elbow. A purple bruise darkened the side of his face. Blood matted his hair. A kind of smile warped his swollen mouth; his eyes glittered.

'You lay us a false trail, Brogan,' Jeb said. 'I'll have you swinging by the neck faster than you can say your name.'

'Bring me water,' Brogan insisted. 'I'll tell you where it is.'

'I ain't listening to this,' Jeb said. 'I'm gonna get those horses harnessed right now.'

He pushed past Ellie and strode down the steps.

'Wait,' Brogan said.

Jeb ignored him and lifted the harness off the side of the wagon. He untied one of the horses and led it over to the cart. He patted its neck and whispered in its ear, just as he always did, as he backed it between the shafts.

'We divided the gold into three.' Brogan's voice cracked.

'Me and Bill took our shares. The rest of it we left.'

'He's lyin',' Jeb said. 'Why would they leave Pa's share?'

'I'll fetch him some water,' Tom said.

He stood up and stepped into the saloon. The broken glass crunched under his boots. Ellie kept her rifle pointed at him.

Tom held a ladle of water to Brogan's mouth. The swelling meant that half of it splashed over his chin.

'You got to untie me,' Brogan said. 'I promise you this is the truth.'

'Don't you get it?' Jeb said. 'You

killed my pa. I ain't never going to untie you.'

'Ellie,' Brogan said. 'Listen to reason.'

'How can we trust you, Brogan?'

Brogan considered. 'All right. I'll trust you. I'll tell you where your pa's share is first. Then you untie me.'

Ellie looked at Jeb. Jeb shook his head. 'You saying you didn't divide it up?'

'We never intended all that to happen,' Brogan said. 'It was dark. We were spooked. When we realized we'd shot Elizabeth, Bill wanted to put the gold back in the ground and run. I'm telling you the truth.'

Tom clutched the side of the wagon.

'All these years,' Tom said. 'You've smiled at me every day. Bill too.'

'How could we tell you, Tom?' Brogan said. 'We did all we could to make it up to you. We looked after you. We were generous.'

Tom turned his back on Brogan and climbed slowly back up the steps to his chair on the porch.

'Harness up the horses, Jeb,' Tom said. 'I want to see him hang.'

'Wait,' Brogan shouted. 'It was Bill. He went nearly crazy. He said Hank Deeds's share was blood money. We could never touch it. Only way I could calm him down was if I promised not to touch it. Told me he'd confess everything to you, Tom, and drag me down with him if I laid hands on a nickel.'

'Where is it?' Ellie said.

Brogan hesitated.

'Under the floor of the saloon. Buried it with my own hands.'

Jeb dashed inside. With knives that he found in the kitchen he began to attack the boards in the centre of the floor. When the blades broke he found tools from the storeroom at the back. It didn't take long. He scattered the boards and left gaping holes like dark patches across the floor.

At last he gave a triumphant cry. Seconds later he heaved an old Butterfield strongbox out onto the porch.

'See,' Brogan called. 'I kept my part of the bargain.'

'It's locked,' Jeb snarled.

'Bill insisted,' Brogan said. 'Said we weren't never to touch it.'

Jeb unholstered his .45 and held the barrel over the lock.

'Wait,' Brogan shouted.

Jeb fired. The vultures exploded into the sky in a confusion of beating wings. The terrified ponies reared up, leapt forward and jerked the wagon after them. Brogan and Gifford were flipped into the air. Their necks cracked like gunshots. When the hanged men's shoulders smashed into the pillar of the upstairs balcony, the cart juddered to a halt.

The bodies spun on their ropes, bumped against each other and eventually became still.

13

'What's going on?'

There was a shout from the far corner of the square; two men ran towards the saloon, .45s in their hands. Ellie caught sight of them and ducked inside. Jeb and Tom gaped at the hanged men and failed to hear the shout. The bodies turned as gently as wind chimes.

'Hey. Who is that?' one of the men shouted.

It took a second for Jeb to focus. It was Brett and Johnny Gifford, their clothes, faces and hands caked in trail dust.

Brett fired. Jeb threw himself face down on the porch and went for his gun. Still running, Brett yelled something and fired again. Jeb loosed off a shot. Brett dived to one side and Johnny to the other. They rolled over, stumbled to their feet and hurled themselves towards cover on different sides of the square.

Without taking aim, Johnny turned and shot two quick rounds. Jeb fired back. The impact of the bullet made Johnny's body spin as though the wind had tossed a coin. He fell face forward in the dirt.

Brett kept low by the side of a water trough. Gasping for breath, he reached for more shells from his belt. Since he entered the square, all his attention had been taken with looking after himself. He didn't know who the hanged men were; he didn't know Johnny had been hit. All he knew was that Jeb Deeds was on the porch of the saloon and he was going to kill him.

'Been having yourself a necktie party, Jeb?' he called.

Brett pushed the shells into the chamber of his .45.

'This is justice,' Jeb shouted. 'Long overdue. I just hung your murderin' pa.'

Brett couldn't tell if he had heard

right. But he heard Jeb Deeds laugh.

'Tom's here,' Jeb went on. 'He knows the reason.'

'Tom?' Brett called. 'You there?'

'On the porch with Jeb.'

Brett couldn't work it out.

'My girl there?' Brett spat the words as though they were dirt in his mouth.

'Was,' Tom called.

'What's going on, Tom?'

'It's true about the hanging. Your pa and Bill Gifford shot Hank Deeds and my Elizabeth years ago.'

Brett laughed. 'Bull. You got evidence for that?'

'Enough,' Tom called.

'Why didn't you put a stop to all this?' Brett shouted. 'Been writing it all up in your record books?'

'They got the drop on me, Brett.'

Brett laughed again. 'Had to wait for the young guys to rescue you. Is that it?'

'Something like that,' Tom called.

'Johnny,' Brett yelled. 'You hearin' this?'

He waited for an answer. Vultures

assembled again on the roof opposite the saloon.

'Johnny?' Brett called again. 'I said, are you hearing this?'

Panic rose in him.

'Johnny?'

Brett bobbed up from behind the water trough and fired three rounds in the direction of the porch. No time to aim. He was distracted by the two bodies swinging over the saloon doorway, heads wrenched to one side, faces purple, blood in their mouths. He hesitated for a second. It was true. It was his pa. Bill Gifford turned beside him in the afternoon sun.

Brett couldn't take it in. His thoughts were jumbled like pieces in a jigsaw-puzzle box. Then someone groaned on the porch. Had he hit Jeb?

What about Johnny? Brett hadn't heard him answer. Where was he? He raised himself far enough above the trough to scan the square. He expected to see Johnny Gifford crouching behind cover somewhere with his pistol ready.

Instead, there was Johnny's body twisted in the dirt a few feet from the water trough on the opposite side of the square. Brett hesitated. This couldn't be.

There was a shot from the saloon porch. Something white-hot burned into Brett's shoulder; agony flamed through him. For a moment he thought he was going to pass out. When he looked down he saw blood soaking through his shirt.

Clinging to the floor of the porch, Tom pushed himself into the saloon. Jeb's face was white with pain; a dark pool formed underneath where he lay.

Inside the saloon, Tom found one of the broken knife-blades. He leaned back against a chair and sawed at the rope which tied his hands. With his hands behind his back, it was awkward work; wet with blood, the blade slipped out of his fingers.

Outside it was quiet. Tom couldn't tell who was dead and who was alive. Brett lay still behind the water trough;

Johnny Gifford was a crumpled heap on the east side of the square. Tom could hear the breath catching in Jeb's throat but how badly wounded he was, he couldn't tell.

It took an eternity to cut through the ropes. Not being able to see what he was doing and with nothing to grip on to, he let the blade clatter onto the floor.

'What are you doing, Tom?' Jeb called.

'Cutting these ties,' Tom said.

'I could shoot you for that,' Jeb said.

'You could,' Tom agreed. 'What would be the point?'

Jeb was quiet.

'Hurt bad?' Tom asked.

'Just a scratch. If he comes for me, he won't stand a chance.'

Tom heard bravado echo in the words. Jeb's voice was weak, too quiet for someone only a few feet away.

'When I get myself out of these ropes I might be able to stop this before somebody else gets killed,' Tom said.

Jeb laughed. 'I'd be our new sheriff's first trophy,' he said. 'Reckon he's gonna let me get away?'

'I aim to see you do just that,' Tom said. He pulled his wrists free and let the rope drop.

There was a movement in the room above. A footstep. Tom heard it clearly.

'Where's Ellie?'

'How should I know?' Jeb said.

'She still got that Winchester with her?'

Tom strode out onto the porch. The vultures arranged themselves attentively.

'Brett,' Tom called. 'I want you to come on out. We got to stop this before someone else gets killed.'

'You armed?' Brett shouted.

'No, I ain't.'

'What about Jeb?'

'He is,' Tom said. 'I'm going to ask you both to throw down your guns.'

'You trust a Deeds?' Brett sneered. 'After what they done.'

'Yes, I do,' Tom said. 'I'm recommending you do too.'

The vultures shifted position along the roof ridge.

'You think on what your options are while I go and check on Johnny,' Tom said. He climbed down the porch steps, headed out into the square and stooped over the crumpled body. He expected to find Johnny Gifford dead.

Johnny's shirt was drenched in blood. His breath was coming in gasps and his eyes were closed. When Tom spoke to him he opened his eyes and looked into his face.

Tom reached underneath him and picked him up.

'He's alive?' Brett called.

'I'm putting him in the saloon,' Tom said.

The afternoon sun hammered down on the square. The dirt under foot was bleached almost white; each step Tom took sent up little pale clouds and dust clung to his boots and the legs of his pants. The air was as dry as paper; the sky was a merciless blue. The shadows between the buildings were black.

Tom laboured across the square with Johnny Gifford's body in his arms. The young man was a dead weight. His head lolled back and one arm hung loose, so that his fingers trailed in the dirt. Shards of pain lanced Tom's knees.

When he got to the saloon porch Tom leaned against the post before he tackled the steps. His breathing was tight; his chest and shoulders burned. Johnny's eyes were closed.

'What are you doing, Tom?'

It was Ellie's voice. The barrel of the Winchester protruded from the upstairs window. The bodies of the hanged men swung in the sunlight.

'Catching my breath,' Tom said.

He let the post take his weight while strength soaked back into him.

'Hey, Brett,' Ellie called. 'Your friend's close to dyin'.'

Brett loosed off a shot. The bullet bit the upper-storey window frame of the saloon and loosened a shower of wood splinters and flakes of paint.

'All we want is what's owing to us,'

Ellie persisted. 'We don't want no more killing.'

'You're supposed to be my girl,' Brett shouted. 'You ran out on me.'

'Never should have got together,' Ellie called. 'Both of us know that.'

As Tom placed his boot on the first step another pistol shot sang through the air.

'I got my Winchester, Brett,' Ellie shouted. 'You know how good a shot I am.'

Brett laughed.

'Got you in my sights right now,' Ellie insisted.

Tom heaved himself up onto the next step.

'Throw out your pistol, Brett.'

White hot pain stabbed Tom's knees. He thought he might fall. His breath caught in his throat.

'Me and Jeb will take what's owing,' Ellie called. 'We'll high-tail it. You'll never see us again.'

'I'm sheriff,' Brett yelled. 'You forgot that? I say what happens.'

As Tom reached the porch with Johnny in his arms, Brett threw out his gun and crawled out from behind the water trough.

'Coming in,' Brett called. 'Put down your rifle.'

He got to his feet. Dust caked the blood on his shirt; his left arm hung by his side.

The vultures shuffled on the roof ridge.

'Where's the posse?' Ellie called.

'Walked on out to the ranch. Left me and Johnny to head into town.'

Inside the saloon the shade welcomed them. Ellie stood at the foot of the stairs with the Winchester in the crook of her arm; Tom lay Johnny Gifford on the floor by the bar and slumped down in a chair; Jeb had hauled himself inside and sat close to the door. Brett stood in the doorway, blinking as his eyes became accustomed to the shadows, and kicked the Butterfield strongbox into the middle of the room.

'This what we're here for?' Brett said contemptuously. 'You think I don't know about it?'

'What are you saying?' Tom said.

'You think I don't know about the stage robbery and how my pa got the stake to build this town? You think he didn't tell me?'

Brett leaned back against the door-jamb. The sunlight fell into the room from behind him and cast his shadow on the floor.

'Johnny knows. The only person who didn't know was you, Tom.'

Brett laughed. 'When Hank Deeds got shot, Johnny's pa wouldn't touch his share. Did you know that? My pa hid it right here, waiting for the day he changed his mind.'

'That's why he kept it?' Tom said.

'At first,' Brett said. 'Then it looked as though he wasn't ever going to change his mind.' Brett nodded to Jeb. 'Go on. Open it. Help yourself to your pa's share.'

Jeb levered himself off the wall. His

footsteps ground broken glass into the floor. He flung open the lid of the chest.

Tom leapt to his feet; Ellie raised her rifle. Brett's laughter echoed round the wooden walls. The strongbox was full of sand.

'Too late,' Brett jeered. 'Years too late. Soon as my pa figured Bill was never going to agree, he took the money himself.'

He pointed mockingly at Tom.

'Paid your salary with it.'

Outside there was a soft thud as a vulture flew down from the roof ridge and landed where Johnny Gifford's blood stained the dirt. The bird shuffled its wings and inspected the stain on the ground.

'You didn't know that, Tom?' Brett said. 'The whole town talked about that robbery and the shootings for years. Everyone had a theory.'

'Town gossip,' Tom said. 'Never listened to it.'

'Well, maybe you should have, Tom,'

Ellie said. 'That's what we've been saying.'

Brett laughed again. He dug his hands in his pockets and leaned back against the wall as if he was passing the time on a summer's day.

'Comfortable, wasn't it, Tom?' Brett jeered. 'You could sit in your office night after night filling in your record books and pretending you were running the town. All the time you had robbery and murder right there in front of you. And you never asked questions about them.'

Brett kicked a piece of broken glass and listened to it skitter across the floor.

'All the time you were giving me orders, you thought you were in charge. My pa and Bill Gifford owned you, Tom.'

Brett stared first at Ellie then at Jeb.

'I'm walking out of here and I'm going to pick up my gun. When I come back I'm going to arrest you, Jeb. If anybody tries to stop me, I'll kill 'em.'

His words hung in the air for a moment.

'Ellie, you can leave by the back door and ride right out of town,' he continued. 'You show your face around here again, you'll end up in jail just like your brother. Folks round here don't take kindly to having their horses stolen.'

Then Brett turned and stepped out into the sunlight.

From inside the saloon, they heard his boots stamp on the porch and down the steps. Through the door, they watched him cross the square. Jeb checked the chamber of his Colt. His face was pale and sweat ran down his temples. The side of his shirt was wet with blood where a bullet had passed through his shoulder.

'Help me up, Tom.'

'You can't fight,' Tom said. 'You can't hardly stand.'

Jeb held out his arm and waited for Tom to pull him to his feet.

'You and Ellie have got horses at the

back,' Tom said. 'Make a run for it right now. You'll be out of the territory before he can come after you.'

'And have a lifetime of ducking and hiding?' Jeb said. 'I killed his pa. Brett ain't never going to forget that.'

'I'll finish him,' Ellie said. 'Could do it with one shot, right now.'

They turned towards the open door. Brett's back was to them. He made his way across the square but his footsteps faltered. Maybe he was more badly hurt than he let on.

'You know what everyone thinks of us Deeds,' Jeb went on. 'Low-down, untrustworthy, you name it.'

'What are you talking about?' Ellie said. 'It ain't the time for this now.'

'Maybe it is,' Jeb said.

Brett was standing still in the middle of the square as if he needed to collect his strength. His pistol lay in the dirt by the water trough.

'I want this thing over,' Jeb said.

Tom hauled Jeb to his feet.

'You looked out for us Deeds kids,

Tom, even though you believed our pa killed Elizabeth. There must have been a time when you wished us to hell but you never blamed us. And I thank you for it. I know Ellie does too.'

Jeb glanced through the open door. Brett was walking slowly towards the water trough; his boots dragged in the dirt. The vulture planted itself where Johnny had lain and eyed him suspiciously.

'But that ain't enough,' Jeb went on. 'You should have figured out what happened. You knew Pa. You knew he wasn't no murderer. He liked Elizabeth. He was grateful to her for the food and clothes she gave him for us kids. You knew he would never have hurt her.'

Tom was at a loss. A short time ago he had a hold on his life, now it was like sand falling through his fingers. He stood accused of a crime he didn't know he had committed.

'I just did my job,' Tom said faintly. 'When Elizabeth died, I couldn't hardly face going out to the house. Didn't want to live there. Brought the timber into town and used it on the sheriff's office . . . '

His voice faltered.

'Couldn't think about what had happened,' Tom went on. 'Our life ended before it got started. That's why I never asked questions.'

Ellie walked forward out of the shadows at the back of the room. The Winchester lay in the crook of her arm.

'Someone who don't ask questions is someone who don't want to know answers,' she said.

Tom stared through the open door. A second vulture landed where Johnny's blood had dried. On the opposite side of the square Brett sat on the edge of the water trough. His shoulders were hunched; he leaned forward, his good arm propped on his knees. The brim of his hat cast a shadow over his face; the afternoon sun glinted off the pistol in his right hand.

'That's true, ain't it, Tom?' Ellie said. 'I reckon you suspected things weren't right. Brogan and Gifford were all over you with promises to help. Brogan let you live free in the saloon. What businessman does that? And the money. Brogan of all people paying you more than was due, and you still didn't ask?'

'I didn't,' Tom said simply. 'Didn't seem no point.'

'Those liars blamed our pa for the murder of Elizabeth,' Ellie said. 'You went along with that. That means you blamed him too.'

'Ellie,' Tom appealed to her, 'I tried to look after you when you were young. I did the best I could.'

'The best you could?' Ellie said. Her voice echoed with scorn. 'You lied to yourself, Tom, just like they lied to you. And you lived with that without turning a hair all these years.'

'Ellie,' Jeb interrupted. 'He's coming.'

Brett was walking across the square, his hat pulled down low. Each step was deliberate and slow. His left arm hung useless by his side; his shirt was black where the blood had dried.

'Jeb Deeds,' Brett shouted. 'I'm comin' to finish what my pa started. Your pa wasn't worth spit and nor are you.'

Brett reached the middle of the square.

'This is my town now,' Brett went on. 'I'm sheriff. I don't want lowlifes like you round here.'

Inside the saloon Jeb pushed himself off the wall and took a step towards the door. Tom grabbed the gun from his hand and shoved him back. Taken by surprise and weak with loss of blood, Jeb stumbled backwards, missed his footing and fell, bringing chairs down on top of him. Tom marched out onto the porch.

'Put that gun away, Brett,' Tom said. 'There's been enough killing.'

'Still trying to give me orders, Tom?' Brett sneered. 'Still think you're sheriff?'

Tom started to climb down the porch steps.

'Stay back, Tom,' Brett warned. 'Jeb

Deeds needs clearing out. I'm finishing up what you should have done years ago.'

'We've had enough killing,' Tom repeated. 'Throw down your gun.'

Brett laughed. 'Changed sides, Tom? You protecting the Deeds now?'

'I want the killing to stop,' Tom said.

'Too late for that,' Brett sneered. 'Stand aside.'

Brett raised his .45. Tom stood at the bottom of the porch steps and faced him, his hand still holding Jeb's gun hung at his side.

'I'm sheriff now,' Brett roared. 'Stand aside, Tom.'

Whether it was some disturbance in the square, a flash of sunlight catching the pistol by Tom's side, the vultures ducking their heads, or Tom himself shifting to ease the pain in his knees that made Brett fire, Tom couldn't say. Maybe Brett caught sight of some movement in the saloon window at the edge of his field of vision. Brett fired twice; the bullets punched Tom in the chest, smashed through his ribs and lodged there. Tom remained upright; he swayed slightly. For a moment, Brett stared at him, unsure that his bullets had hit home.

As Tom fell a rifle shot cracked, kicked Brett backwards and splayed his body in the dust. His gun was thrown out of his hand. Ellie stood in the window of the saloon and lowered the Winchester from her shoulder.

14

Ellie stepped out onto the porch of the saloon still holding her rifle. Jeb leaned on her for support, his arm across her shoulders. The vultures beat their wings and shambled up into the air.

As Tom stared up, the afternoon sun formed a golden halo around Ellie's head. She knelt beside him and told him everything would be fine in a voice that made him believe her. Although his eyes were open and he heard everything she said, his breathing was shallow and quick.

'Ellie.' Brett called out to her from across the square. 'Something I got to tell you.' His voice was strained and insistent.

Ellie stayed with Tom.

'You shouldn't have done that,' Ellie said. 'Jeb would have taken him down.'

Tom smiled. His eyes watched her.

He was too weak for words now. *I tried to make amends* was what he wanted to say. At least, that was what Ellie thought.

Smoothing the back of her hand across his cheek, Ellie felt Tom relax. The stubble on the old sheriff's face felt as rough as wire, his cheekbones were smooth and his skin was damp with sweat. His eyes followed her. Ellie had the feeling that he was biding his time, searching for the words and summoning the strength to say them.

Brett called out to her again. Blood soaked the front of his shirt. His voice was weaker this time.

'Got something to tell you.'

Ellie left Tom and went over to him.

'Pa took the gold out of the chest.'

Brett's voice was harsh; his breathing was uneven. The effort of speaking showed in his face.

'He was scared someone would find it. Put it in the bank in Kansas.'

Ellie stared at him.

'Reckoned as long as no one told

you, it would be mine one day.'

'My pa's share of the robbery?' Ellie said.

'In the Town and City Bank under the name of Hank Deeds. All you got to do is walk in there and claim it.' Brett laughed. 'Reckoned if I could get rid of Jeb, I'd have it all. I'd be sheriff and a rich man too.' He laughed again, but this time the laugh caught in his throat and turned into a cough. He tried to hold it back and his chest bucked with the effort. Blood filled his mouth.

Ellie turned to Jeb then. She sat him down on the porch steps, tore a strip from her petticoat and bound his shoulder tight. For the moment his face was pale and lined with pain, but he was strong. The bullet had passed through; he would recover.

As the afternoon light softened into evening, Ellie went between Tom and Brett where they lay on different sides of the square. She took water to each of them and held the canteen to their lips while they drank. She sat with them and spoke to them. The sound of her voice seemed to reassure them, though oftentimes they were too far gone to understand what she said.

At dusk, the posse arrived with horses for Brett and Johnny Gifford. They were appalled at what they found. Leaderless, they didn't know what to do. Ellie explained everything that had happened, truthfully and without emotion. She answered all their questions.

The men cut down Brogan and Bill Gifford and laid them in the cart. They brought Johnny's body out of the saloon and set him down beside his father. Some of them sat with Brett and talked to him. Others were unnerved and, when they found that there was nothing for them to do there, headed home.

The vultures were silhouetted against the dying light like hunched black angels. Brett died in the night.

At dawn, Tom rallied. Ellie had eased a folded coat under his head and covered him with a blanket. His eyes were bright; he asked for water.

'You were right,' he said. 'I should have stood up to Brogan. Reckon Bill would have backed me up. He felt guilty, that's why he wouldn't spend the money.' Tom's voice was weak but his words were clear.

'No need to explain, Tom.' Ellie smiled at him.

As daylight filled the sky, the townsfolk returned. They were tired after a long night camped out in the desert. Doc Andrews kept to the back of the crowd. Ellie had to explain everything again.

This time Ellie stood on the saloon porch and told them about the gold.

'Now, since the Town and City Bank went bust years ago, that gold don't belong to nobody by my reckoning.'

The crowd shifted uneasily. They could see what had happened, but to stand here and be lectured by a Deeds was something they were unused to.

'That gold is in the Deeds's name,' Ellie went on. 'It wasn't come by honestly, that's for sure. It made a fortune for Mayor Brogan and Bill Gifford. You all know how luxurious this saloon is; you all know the size of the Gifford spread.'

'Didn't do 'em no good in the end,' someone shouted.

'That's my point,' Ellie said. 'There's a chance to do some good here.'

* * *

The graves were dug outside town near the river road. Everyone came to the burial. There was no minister and no time to send for one so the townspeople spoke the words themselves. Some of the anecdotes were fond, some of them were funny; they were all respectfully spoken. Doc Andrews was nervous. He said he always considered he had known the mayor and Bill Gifford well, but in the light of what Ellie had told him, now he wondered if he had known them at all.

When it came to Tom Rider, Jeb and

Ellie spoke in turn. Jeb told stories about how he had brushed up against the law even as a kid. People respected his frankness and, looking at him standing there beside his sister, saw him in a different light. He was honest and funny and unashamed — a different character entirely from the mean-spirited cattle thief caricatured in town gossip.

Ellie spoke fondly of Tom. She talked about his kindness to her as a child and told what she knew about how he had tried to help her wayward father. She even talked about his strained relationship with Brett and how Brett had resented him and was jealous of the sheriff's badge.

Finally, Ellie recounted the events of Tom's last afternoon. She described how he had snatched Jeb's gun to stop him using it and how he had gone out into the square.

'I shot Brett,' she said. 'But I was too late. He had already fired twice at Tom at point-blank range.'

A breeze moved in the mesquites above them. The mourners were silent and still. They had not expected a confession so openly made. The honesty Ellie Deeds and her brother had shown impressed them and made them consider how they had misjudged them in the past. They listened attentively as Ellie went on to tell them what, if Brett's story were true and there really was gold in the bank in Kansas, she intended to do with it.

Epilogue

One Year Later

Ellie stood at the doorway of the new school building. It was a bright morning. The air was warm and a few sketches of cirrus clouds lay high in the pale sky. The timber-frame building had been put up on a vacant lot on the town square a few doors away from the sheriff's office. Ellie was waiting to welcome the children on their first day.

Inside, the schoolroom smelled of new-planed wood. There were rows of pine desks and benches, a teacher's desk and chair and a chalkboard. Ellie was proud of her achievement. Jeb had overseen the construction of the building and when his shoulder mended, set to work making some of the desks. Ellie had never seen him happier. He enjoyed the work and basked in the approval the townsfolk gave him for it.

Founding the school had been Ellie's idea. She had always wanted to be a teacher. As a girl, she had taught Jeb his letters and listened to him read every night in exactly the same way as Annie Gifford had taught her. She watched him scratch out awkward capitals on pieces of slate and sat patiently while he sounded out new words from whatever book or old newspaper page she could find for him. She lavished praise and encouragement on him whenever she could.

When Ellie had tried to teach her father to read and write, she had more of a problem. To give Hank his due, he started down the road to literacy full of good intentions. But he had to climb this mountain after a long day's cowboying; taking instruction from his precocious young daughter when he would rather be in the saloon wasn't easy for him. He never managed much more than to recognize and write his own name, and he argued with Ellie that these were all the letters he needed.

With success with Jeb and failure with her father behind her, for years Ellie nursed a secret ambition to be a school-ma'am. She longed to wear a starched overall and have her long hair pinned up in a bun and to hear rows of children chant their letters on her command. But when she and Jeb discovered that there really was gold in the Kansas bank and her dream had the chance of becoming reality, she changed her mind.

How could an orphaned ranch girl who had spent every day of her young life struggling with domestic chores presume to be a teacher? Ellie didn't know anything. She had only been outside El Cobarde twice: once when she and Jeb holed up in a cave on the Trans Pecos and once when she went with him to the bank in Kansas. The only things she could teach anybody were how to read, write and make sure they got the correct change at the store.

Ellie was convinced the children of El

Cobarde deserved better, so she placed an advertisement in the Kansas newspaper.

Oliver Berkeley, the new teacher, was inside the schoolroom now. He was a gentle-mannered, serious young man who carried a briefcase of books with him wherever he went. He had brought with him his own copy of a many-volumed encyclopedia which he displayed on a shelf specially made by Jeb at the front of the classroom. He also brought with him a large globe that showed all the countries of the world in different colours; he gave it pride of place on the teacher's desk.

Oliver was able to pinpoint for Ellie exactly where El Cobarde was in the world and described how, all the time they were speaking, the world was rotating through infinite space. The depth of Berkeley's knowledge together with his enthusiasm for imparting it overwhelmed Ellie and also made her feel slightly sick. She gave him the job on the spot.

Lawrence Carter came up to her, notebook in hand.

'Care to give me a quote, Sheriff?' He smiled at her. 'The readers always want to know what you have to say.'

'Just say how pleased I am to welcome Mr Berkeley,' Ellie said modestly. 'The opening of the school marks a new beginning for El Cobarde. With good schooling, the new generation will make the town a truly decent place to live.'

Lawrence finished scribbling in his notebook.

'That's a fine formal comment, Ellie,' he said. 'The readers will like that.'

He smiled mischievously. 'Now, how about letting me write that profile? You've been fobbing me off for months.'

'I don't know,' Ellie said.

'The townsfolk petitioned the governor,' Lawrence said. 'They chose you. They petitioned for a pardon for your brother too. They want to know how you're getting on.'

246

From across the square, a boy and a girl approached them, hand in hand. Their faces were clean and their hair was combed straight but the little girl's cotton shift and the boy's shirt were faded and patched. They lingered uncertainly by the entrance.

'Ma'am,' the girl said. 'Me and my brother are starting school today. Do you reckon we should go on inside?'

Ellie smiled kindly at them.

'I should wait right here,' she said. 'I reckon Mr Berkeley will be out shortly.'

Both pairs of eyes were fixed to the tin star pinned to Ellie's shirt.

'You kids from out of town?' Ellie said.

'Our pa works out at the Lazy T,' the girl said.

'Ain't that what they call the old Gifford place?' Lawrence said.

The girl shook her head. 'Don't know,' she said solemnly.

'We used to call it the Gifford place when I lived there,' Ellie said.

The children grinned. 'You lived on

247

the Lazy T like us, ma'am?' the boy said.

The girl rounded on him crossly.

'You know she did. Pa told us. He said Sheriff Deeds is the best thing that's ever happened to El Cobarde.'

THE END